BEIBH
QUEST

€2

Best wishes

Shirley Gault.

Published by David J Publishing 2016
Copyright © Shirley Gault

This book is a work of fiction and as such names, characters, places and incidents either are products of the author's imagination or are used fictitiously. Any resemblance to actual events or locales or persons living or dead is entirely coincidental.

The right of Shirley Gault to be identified as the author of this work has been asserted by her in accordance with the Copyright, Designs and Patents Act of 1988.

All rights reserved, including right to reproduce this book or portions thereof in any form whatsoever.

First David J Publishing edition 2016
www.davidjpublishing.com

Cover Design: Copyright © Jacqueline Stokes
www.yannadesignstudio.co.uk

A CIP catalogue record for this book is available from the British Library
ISBN: 978-0-9934591-8-4

Also By Shirley Gault

In the Midnight Hour
Another Time Another Place
Reflections Two
Reflections

Dedication

To my family and friends for having
faith in me and keeping me sane

BEIBHINN'S QUEST

by
Shirley Gault

DAVID J PUBLISHING

Chapter 1

Scotland 1996

ANGUS STRETCHED AND SLOWLY OPENED his eyes to greet the morning sunlight streaming in through a gap in the pulled curtains; he looked at Sarah still asleep by his side and marvelled at his good fortune having her as his wife.

A small lock of hair rested gently on her forehead, and he silently reached out and moved it off her face. She stirred.

"Morning already?" she sleepily slurred, before turning over and snuggling into the soft feather down pillow.

He smiled; she never was a 'morning person'.

Carefully he rose from the bed without disturbing her further, reached for his dressing gown as his feet fumbled their way into his slippers. He stealthily crept from the bedroom and made his way to the kitchen.

The sun bathed the room in brilliance as he switched the kettle on and prepared his first kick of caffeine. He looked across the lawn to his former home and surgery and beyond that the breathtaking views of the loch bathing in the morning dew.

He felt truly blessed in having such a wonderful family and home in the most idyllic location he could imagine.

When his father Duncan had died last year he was prepared to give up the practise and take early retirement. Much as he loved his work it was just too much for one person to run efficiently. Then Caitlin, his wonderful daughter suggested she and her husband Steven could give up their positions in St. James's Hospital in Leeds and move to Scotland and become G.P.'s. Angus was overjoyed as he knew Duncan would have loved this scenario.

The move from Leeds to the Trossachs went smoothly and the two doctors settled in to their new positions without a hiccup. Angus kept his hand in, albeit on a part time basis, and they worked really well together.

More importantly the patients had taken to the new set up with no complaints whatsoever, but then hadn't they known Caitlin all her life and they were happy to welcome her and her new husband into the village with open arms.

He turned as Sarah entered the kitchen.

"Sorry for wakening you, hen!"

"I should have been up earlier. I want to go into Glasgow today. You do remember Marcy and Brian are coming for the weekend? And possibly Philip and Beibhinn?"

"Surely Philip and Beibhinn will be staying with Caitlin and Steven? Why would they want to stay with us old fogies?"

She laughed.

"The kids have the decorators in! Had you forgotten? So they will have to put up with the old fogies this visit!"

"Ah, the decorators! Yes that had slipped my mind, and not before time! I don't think any redecorating has been done since Mum died; Dad being a typical Scot didn't believe in spending money unnecessarily. I bet Dad would approve of anything Caitlin decided to do; he absolutely adored her." Sarah smiled at the unsaid words. "Even though she wasn't his flesh and blood," added Angus.

"Yes," said Sarah. "Duncan never questioned Caitlin's parentage, just accepted her as a beloved granddaughter."

Angus poured the coffee and gave her a hug.

"I'll have today off and we'll breakfast on the way into Glasgow, what say you, my love?"

"Sounds wonderful, we'll make a day of it," she replied.

"By the way Sarah, did you say possibly Philip and Beibhinn? Is that not definite?"

"Apparently they have a management meeting in London on Friday, so depending on how that goes will determine whether they arrive here Friday evening or Saturday."

"No word of a big day for them yet? It must be two years since they got together?"

Sarah laughed as she ushered him towards the door.

"Right, Mr. Matchmaker! Off for your shower and less of the gossip or we'll never get to Glasgow today! We'll hear all the news from Marcy and Brian when they arrive tomorrow."

London

What on earth can the directors want to talk to us about? And why both of us together? Could it be after two years they don't approve of office romances?"

"One question at a time, pet!" chortled Philip. "It could be quite a simple management meeting or an update on client figures, plus we are only assuming it is a board meeting with all directors. Let's cross our bridges when we come to them; and lastly when did we ever let our personal lives interfere with our business life, too professional, we are." At this he gave her a hug. "Come along darling, calm down, time to get some answers," he said looking at his watch.

The boardroom where their meeting was being held was quite dark and austere. Although housed in a modern building it was furnished more in the style of the founders of the company over a century ago.

Beibhinn sat beside Philip at a large oval table, more like a mirror, she thought, with its highly polished surface; she felt the rigidness of the leather upholstered Chippendale chair, like a straightening rod at her back.

Their immediate manager, Harvey James, entered the room, followed by his P.A., Iris Jenkins, notebook in hand. They both got on very well with him and had socialised with him and his wife on a few occasions.

"Thank you both for attending at such short notice. I appreciate you have a trip to Scotland planned for the weekend so I'll keep this meeting brief."

More of a one to one, or one to two, pep talk, thought Philip relaxing in his chair,

He could sense Beibhinn doing the same.

"The fellow directors and I feel you two with your excellent work records would be the perfect pair to help set up the company's latest office. We don't need your answer right now, but we need to get this up and going as soon as possible, so we would appreciate an answer by Monday. That is the reason I wanted this meeting today; it will give you both the weekend to ponder over it and before you ask, the new office will be in Belfast. With the Good Friday agreement seeming to be going smoothly we want to get in at the start of what we think will be a very lucrative set up, and word on the grapevine is the Americans feel the same, so let's beat them to it! We have already had a recruitment drive and the take up has been excellent, so much talent to choose from and I really feel with your help we could have the perfect 'Dream Team'."

One of Harvey's favourite quotes 'The Dream Team', thought Philip.

"I know what you were going to say Philip, but just bear with me. To get the dream team up and running before our American friends get established, we need you both to train them in our ways and procedures. So away you go, think carefully; it will be a year's secondment, with a very lucrative salary increase plus an outstanding apartment on the Lagan. OK? See you both on Monday at 10am."

At this he rose and left the board room followed by Iris, still writing as she walked.

Philip turned to Beibhinn, saying, "Well now, that is a turn up for the books and no mistake! Shall I give him our answer now? Then we can go and enjoy our break in Scotland."

"Philip, I'm speechless! It has always been my dream to go to Ireland, but to be paid for the privilege; well that is the icing on the cake! Yes, yes, yes! Tell him yes now!"

The tears of happiness were spilling down her cheeks. She rose and gave him a hug but suddenly felt a stiffness that caused concern.

"Philip, what's wrong? Aren't you excited too?"

He held her apart and looked at her glowing face.

"Beibhinn, we're obviously on different wave lengths. No way would I want to go to Ireland, let alone live and work there! Just think what the I.R.A. scumbags did to Uncle Phil and do you honestly think I would accept this offer?"

She was visibly shaken.

"Things have changed, Philip, it isn't as if we were in the army, as Uncle Phil was. We would be there on business and helping the economy by employing locals, a different situation entirely! At the same time I could research my roots and perhaps find my father's grave. Do you not realise how important this is to me? My father was a victim of the troubles too!"

Philip shrugged his shoulders, sighed and moved her towards the door.

"Let's not fall out over this; we don't have to give an answer until Monday morning, so let's enjoy our weekend. It will be so good to see Steven and Caitlin again. What do you say? Truce until Sunday?"

She hugged him again, and this time he responded.

Chapter 2

IT WAS A BREATHTAKING AUGUST morning at the loch side; the sun was still low in the sky, the birds were singing and the fish were kissing the surface of the waters. Caitlin and Beibhinn were strolling along the narrow path behind Steven and Philip.

"The twins love a good catch up," said Caitlin. "It's good to see they are still close even though living so far apart."

"And possibly more miles will be between them if Philip agrees to the move we have both been offered," Beibhinn replied mysteriously.

"Do tell, Beibhinn! What little secret have you both been hiding? Are you thinking of going back to Tasmania?"

"Oh no," she giggled. "Well not just now, although I do miss being there and I really miss my friends, especially Uncle Dub, yes I do miss him so much. Philip is probably telling all to Steven now, although we had agreed not to discuss the situation until Sunday, but hey what is a day between friends?" she shrugged.

With that she continued to tell Caitlin about their meeting with Harvey and his proposition and how she really wanted to go to Ireland and how Philip really did not.

Caitlin listened intently before saying, "Have a word with Mum. She worked in the Province before marrying Dad and settling back here, although when she was there it was at the height of the 'troubles', so it should be a lot safer now. That was where she first met Brian, or Stewarty as you all call him. They worked together on a cross community project. It was also how she met Phil, my biological Dad, but then that is another story. Mum hasn't always been a B&B landlady; she qualified as a psychologist and was a pretty good one by all accounts."

"What a coincidence," retorted Beibhinn. "My mother was also a psychologist, which is possibly why she was such a good 'Agony Aunt' on the local radio station. When she arrived in Hobart from Ireland, not realising she was pregnant with me, Uncle Dub gave her a job in HT1212 radio station and she stayed there until she died. My father Brian Sweeney was a victim of the troubles and when his Aunt Sally offered Mum a home with her, she had no hesitation in accepting, she was so glad to get away from all the bad memories that Ireland had for her. Aunt Sally was a truly lovely lady."

"So, was Uncle Dub, Aunt Sally's husband?"

"No," she laughed. "Just a very good family friend and always an uncle to me. He took Mum's death very badly. She had a heart attack at the station and he found her. Terrible times."

She wiped a tear from its travels down her cheek.

Round the next bend on the path the 'Travellers Rest' came into view. It was a typical little country pub and it was here they had arranged to meet up for lunch with Sarah, Angus, Marcy and Brian.

Philip and Steven turned to the girls. "Come along and stop dawdling and gossiping or it will be tea instead of lunch we'll be having," they joked.

Steven gave his brother a pat on the back, saying, "I don't know what these ladies find to chat about."

"You weren't doing too badly yourselves," chided Caitlin. "Chatting away in a wee world of your own."

Lunch over they decided to have a trip on one of the many pleasure boats on the Loch. It was a lovely afternoon, not too warm, and the slight breeze coming off the loch was welcoming. They all sampled a wee 'tot' of the local single malt before disembarking and heading back to Glenside.

The four younger members of the party headed for the sun loungers on the lawn, while Brian and Marcy decided to have an afternoon siesta, tired after the long journey last evening.

"Dinner will be at 7.30. everyone," said Sarah as she and Angus made their way to the kitchen for a caffeine boosting coffee.

"Any word of you two setting the date yet?" asked Steven as he sprawled out on the sun lounger.

"You mean a date for our wedding?" Philip sat up on his lounger and directed his question at Beibhinn.

"That's really up to 'her ladyship'. If she forgets about gadding off to Ireland perhaps it will be sooner rather than later."

Beibhinn could feel the colour rise to her cheeks. She really did not want to discuss this subject in front of Philip's family, but she rose to the bait.

"If you want it sooner, Philip, perhaps you haven't worked out how financially beneficial it would be for us to move to Ireland for a year. The wedding expenses would be well and truly taken care of, what with extra salaries and bonuses at the end of the secondment; you call yourself an accountant Mr. Blackwell? Shame on you!"

Caitlin laughed trying to lighten a potential assassination of words between their two friends.

"Let's walk down to the village and have a little aperitif before dinner, and leave heavy conversations until later?"

"Sorry, Caitlin, we shouldn't air the 'dirty linen' in public. Yes good idea, let's go to the pub."

Philip agreed with Beibhinn and added his apologies as the four friends headed for the village a few hundred yards away.

Chapter 3

PHILIP BLACKWELL, YOU ARE A male chauvinist pig!" Did Beibhinn really say that antiquated nonsense to him? Two weeks later he could still see the fire in her eyes as this venom poured from her lips. His quiet, agreeable, lovable Beibhinn! He couldn't fathom where it had all come from. A store of expletives buried deep in her unconscious, waiting for the right moment to erupt. Vesuvius had nothing on this girl once she got started! And what had been the 'proverbial straw'? He wrecked his frazzled brain trying to remember word for word their last conversation; more of a war parley, something he would never have envisaged sharing with Beibhinn.

If only this placement in Ireland had never been broached, if only they hadn't been offered the positions, if only...*Oh life could be full of 'if onlys,' if only we let it*, he thought.

"Now what did I say that was so wrong, other than not wanting to go to Ireland?" he mused.

"I told her how good life could be if we married right away instead of waiting until she fulfilled her wish of travelling; how I didn't expect her to work, now what girl would argue with that? And how we could travel together in the future after we had reared our family and seen them settled. Now what was wrong with that? How I could see us settled in suburbia, having leisurely dinners, lovingly prepared by her, and discussing my happenings of the day at the office; and how she could have girlie lunches with others as fortunate as she.

"She would be a perfect home maker, just like wives of yore when men were men and women were appreciative! I offered her this on a plate. It had always been my dream of married life from watching old black and white movies on T.V... My Mum being a widow and a business woman was never lucky enough to have this sort of lifestyle, another reason I wished this for any wife of mine. This was when the explosion, from what had previously been my loving caring Beibhinn, occurred."

In Philip's mind he had been a knight in shining armour rescuing Beibhinn, his damsel in distress. He offered her his life, his home, children, a secure future. Now what else could any girl wish for?

Beibhinn, on the other hand, thought at first he was making a joke out of the situation. It was only when he mentioned what he thought was missing from his own upbringing and seriously wanted her to become a suburban housewife, waiting hand and foot on her time warped husband, that her fuse finally ignited. It gathered speed at the mention of the planned family, and finally erupted at his thoughts of treating her to some travelling when her chores of a housewife were finally completed.

Well, sod him, she thought. What a lucky escape she had had.

"Ireland here I come," she sang loudly to herself, and started packing for her trip of discovery.

Coming almost to the end of the M6 and just before the A70 was a lovely stopping off point; the services here were more akin to a farmers' co-operative with lots of fresh produce for sale, and in the café, she looked forward to a well earned cuppa.

She had never noticed the distance before as she stretched getting out of the car; but then she had always shared the driving with Phil. She remembered the first time they had stopped here.

"Soon we will be going into Lonnie Donnigan' territory," Phil had said as they sipped their steaming coffee and devoured the still warm apple tart and cream.

"Lonnie who?" she had questioned.

"I'll have to educate you on the hits of the 50's and 60's," he had laughed; thinking back this should have been an ominous warning that Phil was besotted with the past, in every way!

"Lonnie Donnigan," he had continued, "was the skittle king of the 50's. One of his hits was 'Cumberland Gap' and that's where we are heading when we are refreshed." He had smiled at her, proud of his knowledge. She had refrained from asking about 'skittle'.

She quelled these thoughts. In another two hours she would be with Caitlin, whom she considered to be her best friend, and her mum Sarah, at Loughview. She was really looking forward to a few days with them before continuing her journey to Ireland. There were so many questions she wanted to ask Sarah, knowing she had worked and lived there in the past.

Forewarned was forearmed, her mum had always said. Oh how she missed her, her wit and her wisdom, and the love she had for the country of her birth never diminished.

That was the main reason she wanted to visit the province and to get the chance to live and work there just couldn't be passed up, no matter what Phil thought. She wanted to see where her mother had grown up, in County Kerry. She had been so good in her descriptive storytelling, like an artist with words; and Belfast, although described during its troubles, seemed so welcoming and the people, according to her mother, second to none with their warmth.

So there were some 'bad uns' as Phil reminded her but wasn't this true of many places. He had become such a fuddy duddy with no sense of adventure and deserved to be ignored by her until he realised we were almost into the twenty first century and not still living in Victorian times.

Calm down, she chided herself, feeling her temperature rise at the thought of how Phil envisaged how a good wife should behave. *Forget about Phil until you're in a better frame of mind to set him straight.*

Most importantly she wanted to find her father's grave and that of her aunt, the only sister her mother had; she had also been a victim of the troubles. Yes, once she had done this she would feel complete. She set off again, through the 'Cumberland Gap' heading for her friends in Scotland.

Chapter 4

PAURIC DOYLE WAS STARTING TO feel his age and for the first time in his fifty plus years, a pang of homesickness. He glanced over the letter he had received this morning and a feeling of dread overcame him. He had always loved receiving mail from Beibhinn; she was such a 'newsy' writer, probably in her genes, passed down from Siobhan. Oh how he missed them both. He felt a lump well up in his throat at the memory.

Beibhinn was the daughter he had never had and would always be 'Uncle Dub' to her. How he would change things if only he had the power of time travel, with the knowledge he had now.

He was well overdue a holiday from HT1212 am and perhaps a trip back home would quell his fears. Yes, with any luck he could catch up with friends from his past in a safe environment.

He felt an overpowering need to protect Beibhinn from what she thought of as the mystery of her past, and hoped against hope his gut feeling was wrong and she would be perfectly safe going to work in Ireland.

The warning bells rang again in his head and he just knew he would not be foolish enough to ignore them. For Siobhan's memory and all she had meant to him he had to be sure Beibhinn would be safe and the old scores that had caught up with her mother would pass her by.

His training when with G2 was still buried deep and he would not ignore the signs.

His first priority would be to get in touch with former colleagues in G2, aka Directorate of Military Intelligence (Ireland) or *Stiurthoireacht na Faisneise*. Although not officially active since the 70's he still kept in touch and had helped out on a few occasions, relocating and establishing new identities, Siobhan being one of his favourite projects.

One name Beibhinn had mentioned quite a lot was Brian Stewart, and his first task would be to discover if this was the same Brian Stewart he had liaised with in the 70's when on active service, along with Major Phil, Joe and Harry.

He knew the lads had cover working in community relations with a Scottish girl, Sarah, and a girl originally from the Republic, Siobhan. Luckily he had never met the ladies, so it was easy for him to help out relocating Siobhan when she arrived in Tasmania.

He had left Ireland for good after his last input in an incident where one of his informants had passed on information that saved the lives of people he had worked with.

For a few years he had travelled back and forward to Tasmania and fell in love with the place, and the fact that a job as a presenter at HT1212 AM became available after he had guest presented on a few occasions sealed his fate and made everything fall into place.

His time served with G2, he went on the auxiliary list and agreed to help out in the southern regions when required; it was, in fact, really a job for life, or the life of the 'troubles' if they ever ended.

Until now he had never felt the need to look any of the lads up, however for Beibhinn's sake he had to be sure of all the circumstances.

He smiled as he remembered the camaraderie they had all once shared. If the general population of Ireland had been able to get along as well as the two security services, there would never have been any 'troubles'. They had all worked so well together, two counter intelligence forces with a common aim: peace on the island of Ireland.

Before booking his flight he got in touch with some of the local lads he had last been in contact with when Siobhan had been so brutally murdered.

It soon became obvious his gut feeling was correct and the Brian Stewart whom Beibhinn had kept mentioning was the same guy from his past. It was also most probable that Brian was Beibhinn's father. So the very fact that she was Siobhan's daughter and she had Brian as a father put her journey to work in Belfast a risky business, especially so if the details got into the wrong hands.

Those same people who had sent Terry Yorke to murder Siobhan would have felt very angry at not getting any acclaim for the dastardly deed! Yes, Beibhinn would have been a worthy target and a prized trophy for these low lifes, a target he would need to protect.

Armed with contact details for Brian, he set off and prayed his journey would not be in vain.

Coming in to land at Dublin he marvelled at the many shades of green in the handkerchief-like fields that rolled down to the Liffey, and on to Dublin Bay.

Johnny Cash got it right when he wrote and sang *The Forty Shades of Green.*

"Methinks I have stayed away too long," he mused, and looked forward to catching up with some of his former colleagues. He would stay for a few days before his final destination of Leeds/Bradford.

He got a taxi from the airport to the Shelbourne Hotel, something the old Pauric would never have done; it would have been public transport all the way for him.

Today was different. He wanted to drink in the scenery all the way to St. Steven's Green and didn't want to miss one sip, and every detail would be stored in his memory.

It really was true, Ireland did get under the skin, and no matter how long away from its shores, coming home was like the welcome kiss of a mother for her long lost son.

Chapter 5

"MARCY WE NEED TO TALK."

"Can't it wait until this evening love? I have a lot on this afternoon and two viewers who are very keen to buy the Leeds salon."

"It is rather important, and surely the estate agents will handle everything to your satisfaction?"

"Right! I can give you half an hour and then I really must go. This sale means a lot to me; it is the salon I first started with all those years ago, so it is kind of special as I want it to go into the right hands."

"You would think you were talking about a child, Marcy, but I do understand how you feel. Your salons were your babies. Just give me a few minutes then I promise you can be on your way."

It was the end of an era for Marcy selling the last of her salons, but she wanted to concentrate completely on Brian and building their life together. After Phil had died so young she had vowed life was too short to waste. Once this final sale went through, she and Brian would travel and do all the things they wanted to do.

Marcy poured them both a coffee.

"Well, I'm waiting."

"You remember when I was in Northern Ireland during the troubles along with Phil and the rest of the team? Well, we worked closely with a G2 team which was the Irish equivalent of what we were. We got on so well together; we were as one team and one of the guys, Pauric Doyle, was especially close to us all.

"He moved to Australia many years ago and is home for a short break. He is in Leeds for a few days and I have taken the liberty of asking him here this evening for a few drinks and a bite of supper."

"Stewarty! This is what you are keeping me late for my appointment for?" she laughed, "You don't need to ask my permission to invite friends here; this is your home too, darling."

She reached for him to give him a hug and could feel the tension in his shoulders.

"What else, Stewarty? What are you not telling me?"

"No use beating around the bush. Pauric is also known as *The Dub*, or as Beibhinn would say, 'Uncle Dub' and he informs me there is every chance I am Beibhinn's father."

The silence was deafening and he reached out for Marcy, but she pulled back.

"So, her mother Siobhan was your ex girlfriend Siobhan?"

"That seems to be the case, but us speculating here is not going to change things. Go sell your salon and we can chat when you get back. I want you to be here when Pauric arrives and we can both hear the rest of the story together."

Marcy's mind went into overdrive. What other dark secrets would be revealed? She called a cab; she was in no state to drive safely. So much for no more secrets; they would share everything from here on in!

Brian poured himself a stiff single malt. He hadn't been aware back then that Beibhinn could have been his daughter, well, maybe a niggle after seeing the likeness to Siobhan, but not knowingly.

Maybe it was for the best that Philip and Beibhinn had parted company; was it entirely legal for step-siblings to marry?

It was another thought to put to Marcy when she returned, he reckoned, sipping at the golden liquid.

Chapter 6

Leeds

PAURIC CHECKED INTO THE HOLIDAY Inn in Leeds, he was starting to enjoy this hotel lark; he hadn't stayed in one for years and now two in as many days. It would be so good to catch up with Brian later, and he was so glad they had chatted on the 'phone before the face to face meeting.

At least nothing will surprise Brian tonight now that he has been told the reason for Dub's visit and the shock of disclosure will have settled down by the time they meet up later, thought Pauric. He had also had a chat with Joe, sounding more like a grown man now than the boy he had been when last they met; and through him had been told about Phil's demise after many years in a vegetative state.

He hadn't managed to get through to Harry as the contact number didn't seem to be working, so many people had mobile phones in this day and age and discarded landlines, and this was progress, he mused!

A get together with all of the team would be good, but first things first, his priority at the moment was Beibhinn and her safety, and Brian was the obvious choice for any information he should have...

He knew there would be no chance of seeing Beibhinn here in England at the moment as according to Brian she was staying with friends in Scotland for a few days en route to Ireland.

Meanwhile he had put out a few feelers to the current team in the Province, trying to gauge how safe it would be for her to live and work over there. Hopefully he would hear some word back from them before Beibhinn set sail for Ireland.

Scotland

Excitement welled up in Beibhinn at the thought of at last visiting Ireland, the land of her forefathers and one her mother had talked so fondly about. The fact that her father had been killed there in the troubles never put Siobhan off the place, in fact it always had a place in her heart, and her enthusiasm for it had transferred to Beibhinn.

She had meant to stay longer with Steven and Caitlin, but they were so busy with their G.P. practice, and at times she felt she was a distraction, although they made her feel so welcome. Sarah and Angus had been great company too and they all felt like extended family to her, she really had enjoyed her visit, but she felt it was time to leave.

Sarah gave her many tips about living in the province and told her to be careful where she went and who she confided in, in fact she told her least said about her background the better, which was slightly puzzling to her! She promised to keep in touch and at any sign of trouble to get back to them and to phone day or night if anything was worrying her.

Beibhinn could not understand all the fuss, wasn't the Province now at peace? But she appreciated her friends concerns.

She was booked on the Seacat Scotland, a speedy catamaran type ferry and from Stranraer she would arrive in Belfast in ninety minutes. Such an improvement from the old Antrim Princess ferries which were more akin to cattle boats, Sarah informed her.

After boarding she sat in the lounge and browsed the route she would be taking when she reached Belfast, to her destination. Mary Porter the personnel officer had sent her precise instructions of how to reach her apartment from the ferry terminal, where to collect her keys, the best place to buy food and directions from the apartment to the office. Nothing had been left to chance with contact telephone numbers just in case of mishaps. I don't think she has left anything to chance Beibhinn thought, everything well covered, and this Mary seems like a perfectionist, I think we will get on well.

She thought of Philip, so stubborn and so determined not to take this position offered, with her; this could have been a wonderful adventure for both of us, but obviously his pride means more to him than me, she pondered.

If they were ever to get together again he would have to change his ideas on how a modern partnership should be, and put his Arcadian beliefs on the back burner; he still called married ladies 'housewives'. How chauvinistic!

By the time she had the route to the apartment stored in her memory, the Seacat had docked in the terminal at Belfast and off she set on her Irish adventure.

Chapter 7

MARCY COULDN'T CONCEAL HER amazement at how relaxed Stewarty and Pauric were in each other's company; it was as if they had seen each other twenty four hours ago instead of twenty four years.

Some families didn't have this closeness, she thought, as she prepared a tray with coffee, hot sausage rolls and tray bakes, for the two friends. Perhaps the jobs they worked on together were so intense they relied on each other so much more than other occupations.

Working as they did during the Troubles in Northern Ireland meant they had to trust each other implicitly; it was a matter of life and death.

"Pauric," she started.

"Please call me Dub, Marcy, everyone else does."

"Ok, but what I was going to say there is a spare room ready if you two want to chat into the wee small hours, and you will be most welcome."

"Many thanks, Marcy. I must say we have so much catching up to do that invitation may have to be spread over two nights," he laughed.

"No problem whatsoever, Dub. You're welcome to stay as long as you want, and on that note I will love you and leave you, as the saying goes. Stewarty will show you to the guest room when you finally decide to call it a day."

"I will indeed, sweetheart," said Stewarty, rising to give her a goodnight kiss on the cheek.

"You have a good one there," proffered Dub as Marcy headed to bed.

"...and don't I know it, it has taken years but we finally have made it and I feel so blessed to have her by my side."

"Well, where shall we start, Dub? There are so many questions I need answers to and firstly are you sure the Siobhan I knew and loved was the same Siobhan you worked with and Beibhinn's mother?"

Dub hunted in his breast pocket and pulled out a well thumbed photograph; it was of Siobhan, Beibhinn and Dub, and he handed it over to Brian.

"This was the last photograph we had taken together at a barbecue at the radio station the year before Siobhan's death."

Brian looked at the photo and there was no doubt, this was his Siobhan, slightly older than he remembered, but it was her, and Beibhinn was the double of what Siobhan was in his memory. He nodded to Dub.

"That's her ok, and if what you tell me about Beibhinn's birth I take it I am her father."

"Beibhinn is my reason for this visit, Brian. Her life could be in grave danger if she goes to Ireland and the wrong people realise who she is, and with the startling resemblance to her mother it wouldn't take them long to work it out."

"I don't understand, Dub. Why should anyone want to harm Beibhinn?"

"The first thing you have to know is Siobhan did not die naturally with a heart attack; she was murdered."

Brian splurted his coffee all over his shirt!

"Murdered! How come this was not general knowledge? Is Beibhinn aware of this?"

"No, Brian, and all being well she will never have to. It was decided to put out the heart attack story and keep any publicity from the murdering gits!"

"So who was responsible?"

"Terry Yorke stabbed her and thought he had made a clean getaway, but the sharks did our job for us, long story, but it goes to show that little pack that was also responsible for Major Phil's injuries are still active and that is why Beibhinn could be in danger. What other questions can I help with?"

"Well, Beibhinn is safe in Scotland for the time being but what is puzzling me is why Tasmania? I know you went back and forward to there before finally settling, and to pack up a lucrative job with so many prospects for a job as a D.J. in some god forsaken radio station! For fuck sake, mate, the mind boggles."

"That, my friend, is an even longer story."

"Well, we have all night and I think a couple of single malts might help with the story telling." Brian poured two drinks from the drinks cabinet and handing one to Dub, made himself comfortable on the comfy chair.

"You know a lot about me, Brian, more than most people, but a few things about my early life weren't even known to me until I joined G2 and got a copy of my birth certificate. I had been adopted as a baby and was always aware of this and I must admit I had a very happy childhood with my adoptive parents. However, they died within a year of each other and it was then I decided I wanted to find any details I could of my birth mother. On my birth certificate was the place of birth, Sacred Heart Convent and a mother's name but no father's. I was born to a Sadie O'Reilly of Swords, and that was the only details I had. So I decided to visit the convent and with great reluctance the Mother Superior finally told me that my mother had me at sixteen and I was put up for adoption after two weeks, on the advice of her parents. She had kept in touch with the sisters until my adoption took place and the last they had heard she had immigrated to Australia with her parents. That was when my quest began in earnest, but I was so lucky knowing some of the guys from the immigration department and they helped me narrow the search down to Tasmania, where I finally found my mother, Sally Sweeney."

"You mean Beibhinn's Aunt Sally? Oh my God, this gets more intriguing by the minute."

"Yes, but only Sally and me knew of our relationship and we decided to keep it quiet, more for Sally's sake than mine. I wanted to shout it from the rooftops, but Sally had a certain standing in the community and I didn't want to sully that in any way, so I remained her friend from the home country. After a few visits, paid for by filling in at the radio station. I had been offered the full time Station Manager's job with a few presenting shifts; how could I refuse? Sally was so happy when I finally moved there and as I was still an auxiliary I helped the department out on a few occasions. That is how I became involved with Siobhan. For her own safety after some of her sisters friends had been interrogated at Castlereagh, she was given a new identity and moved to Tasmania."

"They couldn't have got her much farther away, could they?" said Brian. "Why could she not have explained this to me instead of just saying goodbye?"

"Speed was of the essence, mate, and obviously she was briefed how your career would have been in jeopardy if she continued to see you, so in a way she sacrificed her love for you, for the love of you."

"And ended up murdered in the long run," said Brian putting his head in his hands.

"Everything happens for a reason I always think, you possibly weren't meant to be together and just think how happy you are now with Marcy".

"I think that's enough knowledge for one evening, Dub, so let's drink up and have some shut-eye. We can continue with plans on how to deal with Beibhinn tomorrow."

Chapter 8

PAURIC DOYLE WAS TAKING A trip down memory lane, on a certain road he had almost forgotten about, one he had pushed to the far reaches of his mind; looking out of his bedroom window and seeing Marcy and Brian in the garden, deep in discussion and so at ease with each other, was the key that unlocked his memories.

He went back to Dublin, right back to '70 and a break from his duties with G2 at a barn dance held by his adoptive brother for some charity or other he was helping by providing the music and playing at being a D.J. It was a warm summer evening and the craic from the crowd was mighty, all joining in the fun and dancing as though there were no tomorrow.

He noticed a young lady dancing in one of the corners with two friends. She seemed the quietest of the trio, but when they had eye contact she blushed in such a way so alien to girls of that era that he was immediately intrigued and made a mental note to start up a conversation when he got a break. When his brother Henry took over the decks he headed directly for the corner, after setting up two slow numbers and tipping him a 'wink'.

"I'm Pauric Doyle, and you?"

"Ruth Yorke," she shyly answered.

"Would you like to dance?"

She nodded her head and her face was bright scarlet. Her friends silently giggled at her embarrassment.

"Do I detect a Northern accent?" Pauric asked.

She nodded, and said, "I'm just down for the weekend to meet up with my two cousins. We usually have a get together once a month. I think it's important families should stay close, don't you?"

This was one of the longest speeches she had ever said and to a perfect stranger, but he seemed nice, she thought. "And you? Do you live here?" she asked.

'No, I'm just helping my brother out at his worthy charity fund raiser. I live at the northern side of the city, and totally agree: families need to stick together."

They had another two dances and he had to return to his DJ-ing, but not before getting her contact details and the promise of meeting up the next afternoon for a coffee and chat.

The next eighteen months were idyllic. They met up as often as they could and Ruth helped him in every way she could in his quest to find his mother. She rejoiced with him when he finally did so.

They were deeply in love and when he finally decided to go

to live permanently in Tasmania he proposed.

He never disclosed the full extent of his job. As far as Ruth was concerned he was a civil servant and occasionally travelled to the north. She surmised he worked in the Passport Office for some unknown reason and he never corrected her.

On the afternoon she was to give him her answer about going to Tasmania with him as his wife, she arrived at their favourite coffee house in Belfast, late and very flustered.

"What's up pet? You look to be in a bit of a state."

"Can I trust you, Pauric? I mean really trust you; this could be a matter of life and death and I don't know what to do," she said before bursting into tears. Luckily they were in their favourite corner and no one noticed the distress Ruth was in.

"I want to marry you and spend the rest of my life with you and you ask if you can trust me? Come on darling, what's the problem?"

That was when the bombshell exploded in his head. Ruth had overheard her brother and his cronies plan a job and she recognised one of her university friends was in on the act. She detailled how a kidnapping was to take place and where the captors where to be taken and that a lady was to be 'collected' in Whitehead. Her voice quivered as she gave him these details and he reached out for her hand.

"You are not your brother's keeper and you know this cannot happen? When is this to take place? Do you know?"

"Around teatime today."

"Christ Jesus," he exclaimed. "Ruth, go home, forget what you heard and I will ring you tomorrow, Okay? Do you trust me?" She nodded.

Speed being of the essence, he rang Palace Barracks, gave the code word and passed on what he had just been told, then sat back and prayed.

The next day all hell broke loose. He called Ruth as promised, but a strange male voice answered the phone, so he asked to speak to Ruth.

"Ruth will be speaking to no one, Dublin boy, and never to you...so just fuck away off and leave her in peace."

His training warned him to return to his base and report everything that had happened from his perspective in the last two days and making sure to let them know Ruth had been instrumental in saving lives and for them to pass this information on to detectives at Castlereagh Holding Centre.

This was duly done, although for her sake she had to be brought in for questioning like everyone else on their list. He waited a few days and was just about to try contacting her again when he received a 'Dear John' in the post. Just a few words saying they weren't really suited and she had decided to go ahead with her life in Belfast and wished him well in his journey to the Antipodes.

He left for Tasmania the next week.

Back to reality and what ifs. What if she had gone to Tasmania with him? Would that have stopped her brother murdering Siobhan? And had she really decided they were not suited or had she been told to say that? Should he have tried harder to win her over?

He noticed Brian and Marcy had come back indoors. Time to shower, dress and join his friends. What would Brian have to say when he discovered he was the informant, well Ruth really, but via him? Would he understand why he had left for Tasmania without good-byes? And Marcy - how would she feel? After all, Major Phil had been her brother-in-law. Would she maybe blame him for not doing more? Time for all secrets to be made known.

His biggest worry now after he had taken his journey down that particular memory lane, was whether Ruth had been persuaded by her brother to tell all about him and his plans to go to Tasmania, and through time could this have been the reason Siobhan's cover was blown?

There are so many equations to this puzzle and God alone knows if it can ever be solved, he thought.

Chapter 9

Leeds

"BEIBHINN HAS ALREADY LEFT for Ireland," Brian announced unexpectedly.

"Oh my God, Brian, she hasn't a clue what she may be heading into!"

Dub pushed his hands through his hair. Why oh why had she gone early?

"I'm going to get in touch with someone in Belfast and let them know that she is there and perhaps they can quietly keep an eye until we get that stepson of yours to either go and join her or talk her into coming back."

"Not a good idea, Pauric. They aren't even on speaking terms at the moment and Phil is in France licking his wounds."

"All being well, she will be safe enough unless she opens a

can of worms by trying to find out about her father and aunt and where on earth would she start these inquiries? If you were in her shoes, Brian, where would you start?"

"Local police, Register of Deaths. God knows how her mind works!"

"Well, we can only hope she is kept busy enough for the next few days until I get back over the Irish Sea to keep her out of trouble."

"Would you like my company, Pauric? And I know you like being called Dub, but I never knew you as that!" laughed Brian.

"No problem - as long as I can keep calling you Brian and not Stewarty," quipped Pauric. "Think I will head back alone and see how the land lies. Remember some of the old hands may still remember you and that would be two people I would have to look out for! If anything changes I will get back to you and I will keep you up to date on everything."

Marcy joined them and offered to run Dub to the airport as Stewarty had decided to travel to Scotland and put Sarah in the picture.

"Sarah needs to be aware of everything, Pauric. God knows what Beibhinn will unleash – and, really, it puts more than her in jeopardy."

Belfast

Beibhinn had never worked with a friendlier lot of people and she was really enjoying the experience of interviewing prospective candidates along with Mary, the personnel officer.

Mary was really like a mother hen and so proud to be in at the conception of this new branch in Belfast. She had helped

Beibhinn settle in to her new apartment; in fact, she had settled in so well in the last few days it was feeling very much like home.

If the interviews kept on at this pace they should have their quota very soon, she thought. There really was a wealth of talent in the Province and it all seemed to be knocking on their door.

She reckoned she could maybe have an opportunity very soon to start researching her family's history and with any luck visit her father's grave; her aunt's might be more complicated.

Mary was taking her to lunch and introducing her to the delights of eating out in a peaceful Belfast. From what she had been told during the 'troubles' a lot of eating places and entertainment venues had closed, as did the city centre in the evenings.

The Bodega where they went for lunch was very old world, a black and white building which was entered through a long passageway, to the right a public bar and at the end of the passageway a flight of stairs leading to a very homely dining area. The staff was so friendly and chatted away as they went from table to table giving out menus and taking orders in what was a very packed establishment.

"Is it always this busy?" asked Beibhinn. After the formal type of dining she was used to in London and Leeds with Phil this was so relaxing.

"Doya know what ya want yet luv?" asked a pretty waitress, very heavily pregnant and, although busy, the smile never left her face.

"She wants to know if we are ready to order," proffered Mary, not knowing if Beibhinn had understood.

Beibhinn smiled and nodded, then gave her choice to the girl.

"Don't you feel tired?" she asked, feeling sorry for the girl. She obviously needed the money to be working at what looked like a late stage of her pregnancy.

"Not too bad today, thanks luv, not as busy as usual."

"How long have you to go?"

"Two weeks according to the doctor, but I ran over with the last two, so I'm not gonna hold my breath," she said and laughed as she went off with their orders to the kitchen.

"Good grief Mary, poor girl, already two children and working right up to the wire with her third."

"She will probably be back working within a few weeks after the birth," said Mary. "Jobs are not easy to come by and her wage may be the only one going into her house."

"I sometimes think we are not half grateful for what we have," said Beibhinn, more to herself than to anyone else.

After a beautiful lunch they headed back to the office but not before Beibhinn had slipped a £20 into the waitress's hand.

"Buy something for your baby, and good luck."

"Ahh God bless ya missus, you're a wee saint!"

"Saint Beibhinn," laughed Mary. "You can't save everyone on the planet, but a lovely gesture, good on ye."

"Just my good deed for the day," said Beibhinn. "Now back to placing some more needy souls into employment."

Chapter 10

ANGUS WAS IN THE DRIVEWAY of Glenside when Brian drove in. The two men got on very well together and met up with their wives at least once a month. On hearing the car Sarah came out to join them.

"Good to see you, Brian, come in and have a coffee. You must be exhausted after that long drive."

Brian parked the car and followed the two friends into the guest house. After coffee, he started to relate all the happenings of the last few days and Pauric's contribution to the events.

"So Pauric is Beibhinn's uncle Dub," mused Sarah, "and the same Pauric from G2 who you worked with during our time in the Province. We never did meet, but I remember Phil did say that the two groups worked well together."

"We were like a brotherhood, Sarah. Never before or since,

for that matter, have I felt the camaraderie that we shared. Our work was a matter of life or death and we all looked out for each other."

When he told them how it was Pauric who gave the information that saved Phil's life via his friend Ruth, Sarah could feel cold fingers run down her spine; he had saved her also from a fate worse than death. She shivered.

"Oh my God, Brian, the thought of what those bastards did to Phil and what they were going to do to me doesn't bear thinking about, and what Phil went through for the rest of his life…" she broke off, with the tears running down her cheeks.

Angus put his arm around her.

"But nothing happened to you, thank the good Lord, so put all bad thoughts out of your mind. Phil is out of all suffering now, so please try to put those bad memories out of your head."

"If only I could, my darling. It was the stuff that nightmares were made of," she tearfully replied.

"I'm sorry to have re-ignited bad memories, Sarah, think of all the good times we had over there and how blessed we both are now, you with Angus and me with Marcy, happy as Larry," he laughed.

Sarah smiled at him, and said, "You are so right, Brian. Angus is my soul mate, and I don't deserve him, and he's a wonderful father to my daughter."

"*Our* daughter," Angus interrupted.

"And speaking of daughters: Sarah, I think you know what I am going to say?" Sarah nodded. "It seems more than likely that Beibhinn is my daughter, well by coincidences, it is 99% sure."

Angus spoke up, saying "It will be very easy to prove with a DNA test, Brian. I can organise one for you both, if you like?"

"DNA?" questioned Brian

"It's been used for about ten years now to establish parentage and very accurately."

Brian continued, "Thank you, Angus, but I only have to look at photographs of Beibhinn to see clearly she is Siobhan's daughter and as far as I know I was the only potential father. However, if Beibhinn requires proof then perhaps you will set up the procedure? Why it is imperative to make sure Beibhinn is safe in Belfast is the fact that Siobhan did not die of a heart attack - she was murdered."

He could see the look of horror on Sarah's face, and explained how Pauric had confirmed this fact and who the murderer had been and also why Siobhan had been singled out for this treatment.

"They thought Siobhan had been the informant and that was why she had been spirited out of the country and we still don't know how she was discovered so far away and with a good new identity, so you see why I feel guilty. I was the informant with the help of Terry Yorke's sister."

"Terry Yorke?" asked Sarah.

"He was the murderer. He came all the way to Tasmania to kill Sarah and in doing so met his own end. He fell overboard when trying to escape, although he jumped, rather than face the consequences.

"The story was given to the press that Siobhan died of a heart attack while on air and in a small afterthought in some little known newspaper there were a few lines about a man falling overboard into shark infested waters, so there were only a few body parts recovered. The sad part being it was his sister Ruth who really spilled the beans to Pauric and saved the major's life, and probably yours as well, Sarah."

"How did Pauric know this, Ruth?"

"Apparently they were in a relationship for a couple of years, meeting mostly in Dublin when she went down to visit family. I don't think he ever realised she had a brother in the Provos; he wanted to marry her and take her to Tasmania with him but after that terrible night, he received a letter breaking off the relationship. He wanted to settle there as he had been adopted as a baby and had finally found his mother, Beibhinn's Aunt Sally!"

"If this weren't so real I would say you were making this story up as you went along, Brian. I mean, how many more coincidences are woven around our lives?"

"I don't think I could take any more, Sarah. This has been one hell of a journey!"

"So, did Pauric, or Dub as Beibhinn affectionately calls him, ever get in touch with Ruth again?"

"I don't think so, Sarah, but it wouldn't surprise me if he turned over another few rocks when he lands in the Province. He should be there by now and he is most anxious to make sure Beibhinn is safe. If there is even a chance that she is not, then he will try to convince her to come back here to the mainland or Tasmania, if need be."

"Is he going to tell her the full facts of her mother's death?" asked Angus.

"I think he wasn't going to broach that subject unless he had to, Angus, but between us I think she is old enough now to hear the truth and perhaps it will help her understand the dangers that may possibly exist in Northern Ireland for her."

"I couldn't agree more, Brian. She is not a child and even though there is peace there now, there are still some dissidents on both sides of the divide out for trouble. She should be aware of all the facts."

"I have tried to be truthful to Caitlin about my past life and how Angus came to be her 'father' but she had it all worked out before I told her. These kids are not daft, they are adults and deserve to be treated as such, so let's hope Pauric is truthful to her and if not, as her father, that will be your job, Brian."

"Wow wow wow, Sarah, Beibhinn isn't even aware I am her father yet. Poor girl, she has so much to learn in the next few days."

How prophetic those words would prove to be.

Chapter 11

On Mary's advice Beibhinn spent a lunch hour at Belfast's City Hall in their Deaths, Marriages and Birth Registry department, or 'the comings and goings' as Mary had laughingly put it, trying to find out details of her father's death and place of burial. In fact, she thought, any information would be welcome.

The clerk was most helpful and searched but to no avail.

"Do I have this spelling correct?" he asked and went on to spell out loud, "Brian Sweeney."

Beibhinn nodded, "Yes, that is correct, and the year was 1972, but I'm not exactly sure of the month."

She thought he seemed a trustworthy sort of guy so she leaned forward and whispered, "He was killed during the Troubles, if that's any help?"

He whispered back to her, though he didn't know why they were whispering as they were the only two in the department.

"Have you thought of checking with the R.U.C.? They would have records of any deaths connected to the 'troubles' and I'm sure could be of more help to you than me," he explained, inwardly salivating at the thought of the thick roast beef sandwich awaiting him back at his desk when he could get away from this enquiry counter.

"The nearest station to here would be Musgrave Street," he said and then proceeded to direct her to the address.

Beibhinn checked her watch. She would just have time for a quick sandwich and coffee before heading back to work, so Musgrave Street would have to wait for another day; it was tempting to be late back and check the details today, but she was one of the bosses and thought it better to set a good timekeeping example.

She headed for the Skandia, a Scandinavian type restaurant in Callender Street, just across from the City Hall and on her way back to work. It had become a favourite eating place since Mary had introduced her to it a few days ago.

"Any luck with your search?" asked Mary when she returned to the office.

"Not from the registrar's office, but the very helpful clerk suggested I try the police at Musgrave Street for help."

"Oh boy! "said Mary. "That's a place most people avoid and there you go happily walking in. What are you like, Beibhinn! The sooner I get you into the Belfast mould and way of thinking the better."

The friends both laughed at the idea of Beibhinn coming

into the office and instead of saying "Good Morning," saying, "'Bout yee."

There was so much to learn about this place and how she was loving it, thought Beibhinn. She had never felt so much at home anywhere else since leaving Tasmania.

Next morning there were quite a few interviews taking place that she wasn't sitting in on so she grabbed the opportunity for an early lunch and a visit to Musgrave Street R.U.C. Station. Security was very tight around it and after handbag checks and a frisk down by a female office she was shown into a reception area which was bright and welcoming in comparison to the outside of the old Victorian building.

A friendly constable took her details and scratched his chin, "1972 you say, and a Brian Sweeney?"

"My Aunt Sinead also died around this time. I think she was buried in Kerry, but I really would love to find my father's grave and show my respects before returning to Tasmania."

Yes, now that she had said it out loud, it made her all the more determined to return home when her time in Belfast was over. She missed the weather, the people and especially uncle Dub. A feeling of homesickness that she had never experienced before overwhelmed her; yes, she missed home.

The constable turned to a plain clothed lady working at the desk behind him. Probably a civilian clerk, thought Beibhinn.

"Joanne, could you look through the files for '72 and see if there are any details on a death of a Brian Sweeney or Sinead, what was her surname, miss?" he asked turning to Beibhinn.

"Murphy," she replied.

Joanne, nee Porter, felt she had jumped back into the past as she looked at the lady in front of the desk and her fears were confirmed. There stood a living testament that genes could be carried through the generations. This lady was the spitting image of Siobhan Murphy, her friend Sinead Murphy's sister, and this was a quantum leap she didn't want to take because her past was tangled up in this web too.

She took the details from the constable and said: "This could take some time. Perhaps the lady could call back in a day or two?"

She needed time to think. Her life was good now, she was married to a wonderful man who had no active part in the 'troubles' unlike some of the friends she had grown up with and she didn't want anything ruining this, but at the same time this poor girl needed some answers.

The constable looked at Beibhinn, *nice looking girl*, he thought, *and all she wants are some details of her ancestry*.

"Could you come back on Monday? That would give Joanne some time to see if she can find some answers for you."

Beibhinn went back to the office feeling she was getting somewhere at last and Joanne started looking through the files on the happenings of '72. She knew there would be details of Sinead in there, but Brian Sweeney? What sort of Pandora's Box was she going to open?

It was more than her job was worth not to be seen to do this search and really she was never part of any organisation, although some of her friends were. Wasn't this the case for most people during the 'troubles'? The fact she had been brought in for questioning after Sinead's death wasn't even on her files as she had been cleared of any involvement at the time, but the same could not have been said for some of the others questioned back then. Didn't Ruth Yorke end up in a psychiatric institution for a while after her questioning? More to do with her brother, she thought. Oh he was a nasty piece of work, nothing like his sister. Yes, she liked Ruth. Whatever became of her?

Beibhinn had a smile on her face when she returned to the office. Mary looked up from the many files scattered around her desk, saying, "I take it you had some success in your quest today, Beibhinn?"

Beibhinn related all the happenings and how she felt she was getting somewhere at last. Mary smiled, and when she told her how she had decided on her future after Belfast, Mary replied, "Well that little mind of yours has been working overtime. Do I take it that you will not be contemplating a reunion with Phil anytime in the near future?"

"I did love him very much, Mary, but I feel I never really knew him. He has some very archaic views on married life for one so young and I don't think I could fit in with his plans for a 'Victorian' type lifestyle. Being the dutiful stay at home wife is not in my vocabulary," she laughed. "No, my plan is to return to Tasmania, possibly a transfer back to whence I came, if the powers that be agree."

"I think the powers that be would like you to stay in their U.K. set up, but if you have your mind made up… rather than lose you altogether I can't see them denying you your wish."

"If I don't get some work done here I may not even get to stay for the rest of the year here," she said, opening up the in-tray of files awaiting her attention.

Chapter 12

DETECTIVE INSPECTOR PEARL McALISTER came out of her office which was situated at the rear of the reception desk. She walked over to Joanne's desk and lifted up the slip of paper that the duty constable had passed to Joanne.

"Australian lady?" Joanne looked at her with a look of puzzlement. "The lady inquiring about her late father," she continued.

"Oh yes, I believe she is Australian. Gerry could explain more as he was dealing with her."

"But he has disappeared, so who is covering the desk?"

"He has just slipped off to the loo. Told him I would keep my eye on the desk. We're not exactly busy today. Ah, here he comes now. Gerry, Mam wants to know if the lady whom you were dealing with was Australian."

"Thank you, Joanne, but I am quite capable of explaining exactly what I want to know," Pearl said, smiling at Joanne.

"Yes, she was Australian, Mam. Tasmania, she mentioned. Is there some problem?"

"None at all, constable. I heard the accent and thought it was familiar, spent some time there many years ago, before I was married and long before my promotions," she said, more to herself than to them. "What exactly was her query?"

The duty constable related the quest the lady was on and how they would try to help her and also said she would be returning early next week in the hope of some information showing up.

"Did the lady leave any contact details?" she asked, browsing through the information sheet.

"Yes, Mam. She is an accountant with the new firm setting up round by Lanyon Place. Her contact details are on the form and her name, Beibhinn Sweeney."

"…and her father's name?"

"Brian Sweeney, Mam"

She lifted the sheet and her shaking legs somehow or other managed to get her back into her office;

She sat down at her desk and buzzed on the intercom for Joanne to bring her a cup of tea. This was too much of a coincidence. Surely this could not be Siobhan's daughter? She had been told of her old friend's untimely death and the circumstances under which it had occurred, but still she never expected anyone to come looking for the fictional Brian Sweeney. Only Siobhan would have kept her daughter's father's Christian name the same. That woman really loved Brian Stewart, so much so that she disappeared out of his life, as she didn't want to be the cause of him having to give up a career that he loved.

She thought back to their journey together, firstly to England then to Dubai and on to Australia, when the poor girl was breaking her heart, firstly at the loss of her sister and then of the self-inflicted separation from the man she loved and had planned to marry.

She doubted Siobhan even knew she was pregnant on that long journey. They had spent so much time together and got to know each other very well in the few weeks in each other's company and she was sure it was a shock when she had discovered she was pregnant.

I wonder if she had known would she have left Brian so easily without at least sharing the news of him due to become a father?

From what she remembered of the lady, yes for him she would have sacrificed her own happiness for his sake!

She looked over the form again and took a note of the telephone number beside Beibhinn's name just as Joanne came in with her cup of tea.

"Thank you, Joanne, you can have this file back and let me know if you have any luck with your search. It seems like an interesting case."

How interesting you will never know, thought Joanne as she returned to her desk.

She made a pretence of checking back through the files but her heart wasn't in it. She knew all about Sinead's death as it was all over the press at the time and wasn't that when she was brought into Castlereagh Holding Centre for questioning?

Thank the good Lord I had only socialised with the girl on a few occasions and that was always in a crowd, and had only been to her home a few times as well.

Remembering back, she never was that close to Sinead, other than sharing a few classes at Queen's and moving in the same circles with Ruth, mainly that was the height of knowing her. Ruth was more of a friend and even they had grown apart over the years which was maybe just as well.

Wasn't that brother of hers in and out of the Maze Prison like a yoyo? Poor Ruth. Word on the street was that she had had a nervous breakdown and spent some time in a mental institution. Is it any wonder with family like that?

"Any luck with the search yet?" asked the duty constable, looking over at Joanne.

"No, I'll check some more after I get my filing cleared up. I'm beginning to think I'm the only one who does any filing in this office! Just have a look at my desk - it is like 'Maggie Moors'."

Maggie Moors was a well-known second-hand shop years ago in Belfast's Sandy Row.

The time had come for a change of shift and a few of the new crew came through the office to clock in.

"You moaning again, Joanne?" asked one of the guys.

"Just speaking the truth, Jimmy. No one seems to do any filing here only me; the lot of you think my desk is your wee personal post box, just set all paper work down and wee Joanne will put it where it should go, I know where I feel like sticking it…"

"Joanne!" Pearl came out of her office trying to keep her face as stern looking as possible when wanting to burst out laughing.

"Right lads and lasses, briefing in ten minutes in my office, no more keeping the lovely Joanne back from her work."

Joanne decided before looking for any facts for Ms Sweeney she would have a chat with her husband when she got home and seek his counsel. He knew all about her wayward friends from her past and was so proud of her for making something of herself. Being accepted into the civilian side of the security forces proved to the world she was a good one, with no skeletons in her cupboard.

Yes, Rob would help her decide what to divulge, and come to think of it, maybe a visit to the Linenhall or Central Libraries would dig up lots more information than she could.

It's a wonder the lady didn't think of that, but then again, being Australian she wouldn't have known of these two places.

Joanne looked at the clock. It was time for home and a long weekend to look forward to as she had booked tomorrow off as a holiday.

Little Ms Oz may wait 'til next week, she reckoned. If she's waited this long, another few days won't make any difference.

Chapter 13

THE FIRST STAGE OF THE recruitment was complete. Beibhinn and Mary relaxed in the Personnel office. They were well pleased with the staff they had enrolled albeit for a three-month trial, but they were both confident their selection process had picked the cream of the crop; already they were gelling together and starting to be formed into a team with the first instated welcoming the last of the team with anticipating gusto. The sense of excitement at being there at the start of a new project was generating a feeling of unity and loyalty throughout the office, a sense of adventure.

"Well, my friend I think a wee celebration is called for, maybe a few drinks this evening, shall we ask the guys…"

"…and girls," interrupted Beibhinn to Mary's fully flowing conversation.

"Of course. Let's ask them all for a drink this evening, call it staff bonding and we can put it down to expenses. Any ideas for where we should go?"

"Well, firstly I can't see Harvey objecting to that expense. We have recruited what I think will be a great team in half the time he thought it would take us and that was without the input of Philip Blackwell! Just think of the wages and expenses he is saving without having to pay extra to my ex."

Mary stopped what she was doing and looked at Beibhinn,

"That name rings a bell with me, but for the life of me I can't think why. How or who do I know with the surname Blackwell? My memory is getting worse," she laughed.

"As I was going to say, Mary, no use asking me where to go, you are the local and you sure know some great eating establishments, so where can twenty people meet up for a drink in this beautiful city and as for the surname it was quite common in the north of England where Philip comes from."

"Ack, times my head wouldn't carry me the length of me," said Mary.

Beibhinn puzzled over another Belfast idiotism but decided not to ask this time.

"Well, Mary have you decided on a venue?"

"It will either be the Crown or The Duke of York," Mary announced. "I think the Duke of York will be better. We can have a few nibbles with a couple of drinks, get to know each other and if anyone wants some music and a bit of dancing that can be facilitated in the upstairs lounge, and it's just a short walk from here. Tell you what, I'll give them a buzz and reserve a few tables and you check the numbers for me. I hope everyone will be available. Tell them they can leave at four if they want to go home and change."

Beibhinn nodded and went into the outer office and proceeded to see who fancied a get together later. This could be a fun filled night, she thought, surprised at herself for looking forward to enjoying herself without Philip.

Everyone was agreeable and surprised at this treat so early in their employment. The atmosphere in the office was electric.

"That will be twenty going, including ourselves, Mary."

"So, no abstainers then, all the staff from phase one raring to go. By the way, Beibhinn, has Harvey said when the next recruitment will be?"

"It will be after Christmas, Mary. Phase One recruits should be well settled in by then and perhaps leaders from them will surface and help with the training of the new ones. We'll see how this lot settle into our ways and how quickly before we start any more, Harvey's words, not mine," she laughed.

When Beibhinn returned to her apartment there was a message on her answer machine which put a smile on her face. Uncle Dub would be arriving tomorrow and looking forward to seeing her. He would have been here to surprise her today but unfortunately all flights from Leeds were fully booked, so he would be arriving lunch time tomorrow. He was staying with Marcy and Brian and they had passed on her contact details. Oh dear, thought Beibhinn, she really should have been in touch sooner with uncle Dub. She hadn't gotten around to telling him she had broken up with Philip and was intending ringing him over the weekend as she normally did call about every fortnight to keep him up to date; after all he was the nearest thing to family that she had.

No use phoning Marcy's now, she had about an hour to get ready and meet up with her workmates and better no call than a quick few words. They would have all weekend to catch up and she was so looking forward to seeing him again. *Why oh why hadn't he said he was thinking of coming to the U.K.*

Knowing Dub, it was probably a spur of the moment decision. He rarely planned anything or even more rarely holidayed away from his beloved radio station.

Let's hope everything is ok and he is alright, she mused; now I am being silly. Better get ready or I will miss all the fun!

After showering, she decided on a pair of cream linen trousers and a jade green silky T-shirt and slipped on a pair of matching green strappy wedge heeled sandals. It was a mild autumn evening and she was so glad to be out of the 'office style' grey trouser suit, more of a uniform, she wore to work.

The toot of a car horn alerted her that her pre-ordered taxi had arrived, so she grabbed her handbag and a tan leather jacket and proceeded to the road below.

"Duke of York, please," she instructed the cab driver.

"Right ye be, miss. Going out for a bit of a boogie?" he enquired.

"I'm meeting some friends from work. I've never been before but am assured it is a great venue," Beibhinn said.

She was surprised at how at ease she was with a complete stranger but in the short time she had been here she had come to know how friendly these people were. They passed the Albert Clock and he turned the cab into Waring Street; there was quite a bit of traffic and mostly taxies, she noted.

"Quite a busy area," she said.

"This is the hub of the city," he laughed as he pulled in to the side of the road. "I can't get you any closer, but if you just go up to the end of that street and look over to your left you can't miss it."

He held the door open for her, pointing across the road to what she could see was just a small street. She paid him, giving him a pound tip, and bid him goodnight.

As she crossed the road there was Mary in front of her heading in the same direction.

"Hi Mary, wait for me, I don't want to get lost in this maze of streets."

Mary halted and said, "You get lost? Never! Come on, let's have some fun."

Chapter 14

Scotland

SARAH SLOWLY WALKED ALONG THE water's edge. She unthinkingly skimmed pebbles over the calm surface, undisturbed by pleasure boats at the other side of the loch. How many times in the past had she walked these shores looking for answers? And how many times had the tranquil surroundings soothed her mind and made it so much easier for her to make decisions?

She came to a wrought iron bench, needing some tender loving restoration, and thankfully sat down to rest her feet and her mind. She had walked a lot farther than she had intended and with her car parked in Luss, her favourite lochside village, she would have quite a walk back again. This is where Auntie Jean, Uncle Jamie and dear Duncan were buried and after placing flowers on their graves she had done what she usually did when stressed, taken a walk by the loch.

With Brian's visit raking up so many memories she really needed time to herself to think. Angus, being the wonderful husband he had always been and knowing when she needed time, had suggested taking Brian to the village pub for a pre- lunch drink and meeting up with her there when she had enough time to work out what advice she could give him.

She looked at her watch. It was almost noon and time for her to return, without any answers coming quickly to mind. She rose from the bench and at a faster pace than she had come, returned to the car park at Luss.

She left the car at Glenside and walked to the village. It was only a matter of minutes away and she felt the need of a little tipple. *Why, oh why, was life so complicated?*

The two men were sitting in the beer garden, taking the benefit of the warm autumn day when Sarah arrived to join them. Angus rose to his feet.

"Would you prefer to eat inside, hen? We thought we would take advantage of this glorious day to eat al fresco. Dear knows how much longer we will be able to do this; winter sets in so quickly," he said, more to himself than to Sarah and Brian.

"This is fine, Angus. When do you go back Brian? Not that I'm trying to get rid of you," she laughed. "Will you be joining Pauric in Belfast or returning to Leeds?"

"I'm actually waiting for a call from him. When I was talking to Marcy last night she said he wasn't able to get a flight until this morning, so all being well he will be able to talk some sense into Beibhinn and bring her home with him, and thankfully that will be the end of all the drama."

Sarah smiled and nodded. If only life was that simple. When she thought of all the drama that had surrounded their little group from the seventies…had it been recorded in a book everyone would think it was fiction! What with Phil getting beaten to an inch of his life, literally left for dead. and then the ensuing years battling with Parkinson's, Siobhan being uprooted and relocated to Tasmania for her own safety after her sister had been murdered by her cronies in the I.R.A. or Provos, and after a good life there and having Beibhinn, finally being murdered herself! She shivered at the thought of it all.

Brian hadn't come out unscathed either, losing Siobhan thinking she had deserted him and now over twenty years later discovering the truth and finding out Beibhinn was his daughter, then discovering his colleague from G2, Pauric, was the uncle Dub that Beibhinn so lovingly referred to. The coincidences got weirder and weirder - the fact that her daughter had been brought up by Major Phil as his own, that Angus had married Phil's nephew Steven, albeit no blood ties as the twins had been adopted, and Beibhinn almost marrying the other twin brother Philip, until their break-up a few weeks ago over her going to Ireland when he point blankly refused to accompany her.

Oh yes, she thought, *fact is so much stranger than fiction.*

After they had lunch she returned to Glenside to await a call from Pauric.

Chapter 15

BEIBHINN FOLLOWED MARY INTO THE Duke of York and immediately felt the ambience, a step back in time, another era altogether. "This place is magical," she whispered to Mary.

"You'll have to speak up, love, the noise level doesn't get any better, in fact this is quiet compared to what it will be later," laughed Mary.

They spotted the rest of their party at two adjoining booths and separated, Mary sitting with the first booth's occupants and Beibhinn moving in beside those in the second booth; they had decided to do this and swap over after a while to get to know all the new staff members.

Beibhinn nodded to Mary that she would settle the bar tab and went over to the bar and left some money there, telling the barman to supply drinks for the two tables and let her know when it ran out. He followed her over to the tables and proceeded to take the drinks orders.

"There should be some sandwiches and other food which we ordered earlier," Beibhinn shouted to the barman, struggling to make herself heard over the din. "Perhaps you could bring it over with the drinks."

He gave her the thumbs up sign and headed back to the bar.

She then got into conversation with the guy on her right, saying, "This is so historic, I just love old pubs, do you know anything of its history?"

"Well, it's not the oldest bar in Belfast," he said, "but it is more than two hundred years old and the present owners try to keep the décor true to the fifties era. It is very well known here in Belfast and the amount of celebrities that have passed through the portals are uncountable. Have you heard of the Undertones? Or is that a stupid question?"

"Sorry, I don't think I know the Undertones," she admitted. "Perhaps if you'd tell me some of their work…?"

He smiled and continued, "You must know Teenage Kicks? That was a Number One and was recorded not a million miles from here, actually just behind in the Wizard studios. They were signed up by Terri Hooley, another local legend."

He paused and smiled at her puzzled expression.

"He gave them a recording contract," he explained. "When they sent a copy of the record to the BBC's great DJ John Peel, he played it twice on his show, a feat never before or since repeated."

"You must think me so silly," she laughed, "but being brought up in Tasmania I have missed out on a lot of music from the local scene, so thank you for bringing me up to date. You are so knowledgeable. Is local music a passion?"

"Local history is more a passion," he replied, "and it helps me chill after a hard day at work."

"Are you trying to say we work you too hard?" she laughed, "and the journey is only starting!"

"Not at all, I'm really enjoying the challenge of being in at the start. How many of a staff do you envisage having when we really get up and running?"

"Probably upwards of two hundred," she said rising from her seat, "but we are here to relax and have some team bonding, so no more work talk."

She made pleasant conversation with all of the staff in her booth, checking if they needed a refill and sampling the hot sausage rolls as she spoke, and moved round to where Mary was sitting.

"Everyone enjoying themselves?" she inquired.

Mary rose and joined her.

"This is going down rather well I think it was a good idea. Everyone seems to be gelling quite well and I must say the food is rather scrumptious," she said as she sampled another sausage roll.

She had a good look around all the walls covered in mirrors advertising Irish Whiskies. Yes, a great ambience, she thought.

"How is the petty cash stretching?" asked Mary. "Will Harvey be having a heart attack when he sees the expense sheet?"

"I think he will give us a bonus for having the great idea of this bonding session; have you ever seen people who have just met in the past few weeks getting along so well?"

"You forget where we are, Beibhinn, troubles or no troubles the people here are the friendliest in the world and some of the best grafters too. I can't wait to get the whole show on the road; the Yanks won't stand a chance!"

They swapped seats and Beibhinn got chatting to one of the latest recruits, a rather shy fellow who had great credentials from what she remembered. He knew what was expected of him and he would, she felt, be a great asset to the company.

"Well, Barry, are you enjoying the 'bonding' night?" she asked. He nodded. "How do you find the office facilities in comparison to your other positions?"

"Very good," he stammered, "very modern and up to date."

Why did she feel this was the most conversation she was going to get from him? Well, she had tried and with the friendliness of the rest of the staff, he would probably fit in in no time. Nothing wrong with being shy, and his qualifications were second to none. He had the makings of a great manager, she thought, but only if he could conquer his shyness.

"Let's be having you all for a group photo," shouted Mary, having enlisted the help of one of the barmen.

They formed into a crescent with Mary and Beibhinn taking centre stage.

After a few shots they dispersed with Mary retrieving the camera and telling Beibhinn she would leave the film into Lizars camera shop the next morning for developing.

"If you could tell Lizars to pick the best group photo and make a couple of dozen copies - that way we can give one each to the staff and send one to Harvey to let him see the latest acquisitions to his firm, and hope he sees them as his 'Dream Team' of the future."

"Will do, captain," said Mary making a mock salute.

"How many have you had, lady?" asked Beibhinn, laughing at her new found friend.

"I'm on soft drinks tonight, my friend. It wouldn't do to get 'bladdered' - that means intoxicated, by the way - on our first night out with the new staff, now would it?"

"Mary, you're incorrigible, but what a breath of fresh air. I think tonight has been a complete success, what say you?"

"I agree wholeheartedly, and here's to many more great nights like this."

Beibhinn was elated when she settled up the final bill with the bar staff, not as much as she expected. It just goes to show the Irish reputation of being heavy drinkers was not apparent here and, as she had heard them say, the evening was a complete success and the 'craic was mighty'.

She bid them all farewell and went to find her taxi, as many of the others were staying to enjoy the dancing in the upstairs lounge.

She had a very welcome visitor arriving tomorrow and she was so looking forward to catching up with him.

Chapter 16

PAURIC WENT TO THE CAR hire counter at Belfast City airport, collected the keys and, accompanied by a member of the car rental staff, made his way outside. It was a beautiful autumn morning and he breathed in the Irish air, so glad to be back. This part of the world never had the extremes of weather experienced in Tasmania, in fact it never had extremes, full stop.

God's own country was a term he remembered Ruth using on more than one occasion. Why on earth had the memory of Ruth come into his head? Was it being back in Northern Ireland where they had spent so many happy times? Or was he just getting old and holding on to happy memories?

Dismissing the thoughts on arriving at his destination, he thanked his escort for guiding him to the hire car and proceeded to leave the car park and head to the city; it was only a ten-minute drive to Beibhinn's apartment and he was so happy to be seeing her again after all this time. He could only pray she was safe and hadn't got into any of the wrong company that could be so easy to do for a stranger to these parts.

Beibhinn's welcome was second to none; she hugged him as though she was scared he was going to disappear.

"Oh, I am so glad to see you, uncle Dub. You must have known I was starting to get homesick when you decided to visit."

She wiped away the tears flowing down her cheeks and searched up her sleeve for a handkerchief.

"What a welcome. It is so good to see you, too, Beibhinn, and I see you still have the little girl habit of keeping a tissue up your sleeve," he noted, laughing.

"To what do I owe the pleasure for this visit? And how long are you staying? And when do you go back to Tasmania?"

"Hold on! Whoa," interjected Dub. "One question at a time. Do I need an excuse to visit my favourite niece?"

"Your *only* niece," she interrupted.

"I just thought I needed a holiday and talking of being homesick, I was feeling that way, too. It's well over twenty years since I left the old country and what better time to come back? Now I can kill two birds with one stone, visit home and see you." He gave her another hug, so glad to see her safe and well. "Now, tell me all about your time here? How's the recruitment going? Have you made any friends? And where can I take you to lunch?"

"Now who's asking more than one question at a time?" she laughed. "Let's do lunch and we can chat later, you must be hungry having had an early start this morning."

"Where do you recommend now that you're an inhabitant of this lovely city? I bet you know all the good food outlets by now."

She laughed at that as he always teased her when she was back home and how she preferred to eat out than cook!

"We shall go to the Bodega. It's just a short walk away, so you won't need to take the car, and I know you will just love the food and the atmosphere."

His mind went into overdrive. That was a favourite place of his and Ruth's back in the day. Why oh why was Ruth so much in his mind? It was as though she were close by. He could sense her closeness. He was being silly. She was probably married with children and possibly anywhere else in the world other than here. *Pull yourself together man*, he chided himself.

"Lead on, McDuff," he said, helping her into her coat. "Come to think of it, I am feeling peckish."

The Bodega has hardly changed at all, he thought, as they waited to be seated. Being Saturday lunchtime it was very busy, but they had been assured there would only be a short wait for a table.

Beibhinn looked around to see if the pregnant waitress was still here, although by the look of her the last time she saw her, she doubted it. She's probably had the baby by now, she thought. As the staff had said, they only had to wait a few minutes before a table became available.

The waitress who showed them to the table tidied up as they sat down. Still as busy as ever, mused Beibhinn, multi-tasking at its best. They browsed over the menu and Beibhinn selected a BLT. with French fries and Dub decided on a rib eye steak.

"Would you like a drink while you wait?" asked the waitress and they both decided on a shandy.

"The girl who was here when I was last in, the one who was heavily pregnant? Has she had her baby yet?" Beibhinn asked.

"You mean Bridie? She had a wee girl two days ago, a wee dote she is too," smiled the waitress. "She will probably be back in the next few weeks - we need the staff and she needs the money, isn't life crap?"

The waitress moved away and Dub turned to Beibhinn, saying, "You really have settled in here, even knowing the staff!"

"It's just that I worried about her, uncle Dub. She was so heavily pregnant and working away here on an eight hour shift and not a complaint out of her, and she was so near to her time, I'm just glad she has it over her, but it looks like she will have her nose to the grindstone again pretty soon. Sometimes I think we are not half grateful for the lives we have; I was saying that to Mary the last time we were here and she agreed."

"Mary?" asked Dub.

"The firm's Personnel Officer, Mary Porter, a lovely lady; don't know how I would have managed without her in the last few weeks. She is a real gem. She even organised my apartment and has introduced me to quite a few good eating places, and we get on really well work wise, so that's a bonus. We were socialising last night with the new recruits in the Duke of York, more of a staff building stroke bonding night and it really went well."

"Well, it doesn't show today," he smiled. "You must have been behaving yourself."

"I was indeed, had to set a good example and how would I gauge people if under the influence? And I'm glad to say everyone behaved and we had no over-indulgent incidents, which can only be good."

He looked at her and marvelled. Siobhan would be so proud of this little lady; how self-assured and independent she had become, a long way from the child he had lovingly watched grow up.

He had decided to stay a few days and check the situation with his contacts. If they could assure him Beibhinn was in no danger then he would happily go to Dublin to catch up on his friends before returning to the mainland to update Marcy and Brian on what he thought about Beibhinn staying here.

With any luck he would not have to divulge any secrets and would happily let Brian discuss her parentage with her. But the best laid plans can sometimes go astray, and what was to occur on Monday could change the course of his life forever.

They talked nonstop over the weekend and telling Beibhinn he had a few people to look up on Monday morning he agreed to meet her in the Scandia for lunch, thinking that with any luck the news he would receive would be positive and he would be able to head for Dublin on Tuesday.

Chapter 17

AFTER BEIBHINN HAD LEFT FOR the office on Monday morning, Pauric called his friends in Intelligence. So far everything seemed to be going fine, but just to be on the safe side he had an appointment with a Detective Inspector in Musgrave Street RUC Station who had apparently shown an interest in this case.

He drove round by the Albert clock, passed the docks to his left and turned right into Upper Ann Street; across the entrance into the police station was a barrier manned by an armed constable.

He showed his photographic ID and as if by magic the barrier rose to allow him to proceed to the rear of the building. There, he parked his car in the spot marked for visitors. This old Victorian building hadn't changed in years, he thought. It was well overdue a make-over. He walked across to a doorway with an intercom and bell, which he rang as he held his ID up to the camera angled above his head.

A voice came through the intercom, saying, "Press the black button and state your name and business."

"Pauric Doyle and I have an appointment with D.I. McAlister."

The door opened and Pauric stepped into to a bright and airy room that contradicted the austere exterior. A young civilian clerk asked him to take a seat, saying she would inform D.I. McAlister that he had arrived.

Pauric looked around the room. There was a chill in the air. How many poor sods had sat here before him awaiting their fate, he wondered. The décor had changed quite a lot since he had last been here but the feeling of authority still lingered in the air. This was mainly a holding area back in the day for those 'helping with inquiries' en route to Castlereagh. It must have put many a shiver up their spines.

The young clerk reappeared and asked him to follow her. They walked down passed the public reception area and into an office to the rear of the inquiry desk.

D.I. McAlister rose from her desk when Pauric entered and extended her hand.

"Well Pauric, it's been a long time since we last met and what a surprise you being here. Last I heard you were still in the Antipodes."

"Pearl Bradley! Well, I'll be damned," he said as he warmly shook her hand. "You are the last person I expected to see. A change of name and promotion, you have done well for yourself."

"One never knows what life has in store for them from day to day," she said. "I wasn't surprised when you arranged a meeting after seeing Siobhan's double here last week. I take it that's why you are here? This girl," she said, pausing to look down at her desk, "Beibhinn…she is Siobhan's daughter? Yes?"

"Got it in one," he said, smiling. "There's no mistaking the resemblance. That's why I am so worried about her working here. What if she is recognised by the wrong people? She hasn't got a clue about her mother's past."

"Well, I gathered that when she came in here to inquire about a Brian Sweeney. That was the made up name we had as part of Siobhan's cover and her transformation into the widow Sweeney, who had come to Tasmania to live with her dearly departed husband's aunt and unknown to me, pregnant with his child, am I right?"

"Correct, Pearl. I don't think she was aware she was pregnant when she last saw you or she might have been tempted to tell you to let Brian Stewart know he was to become a daddy, and dear knows how many cats that would have put among the pigeons!"

"I passed on the note she wrote to him, after it was scrutinised, you know? It was the most heart breaking task I had to do up to that point and I'm sure they really loved each other; how cruel life was to them and probably many others during the troubles. Do you know if Brian knows that Beibhinn is his daughter? Has anyone been in touch with him?"

"I stayed with him and his new wife in England before coming over here, and yes he knows all the details."

He then proceeded to tell Pearl of all the happenings since

Siobhan's murder and how through pure chance Beibhinn had met Philip, now Brian's stepson, and how because of his uncle Phil's treatment at the hands of the Provos he hated this place with a vengeance and had refused to come here to work with her.

"Unbelievable," she said as he finished relating the sad tale; even talking about Siobhan had brought tears to his eyes.

"How is the situation here at the moment? Has peace really come to the province?"

"Well, it's not for want of trying by the majority of folk, but there are the few who want to keep the violence going. These dissidents can stir things up now and again and they do keep us on our toes. Security is laxer in everyday living but we cannot afford to be lax, it's more than our jobs and lives are worth!"

"I was surprised by the strength of security as I came in today, but if it makes for safer working conditions, that's all to the good."

"Have you told Beibhinn yet that Brian Sweeney is only a figment of someone in the distant past's imagination? In fact, does she know anything of her mother's and real father's past? You do know that she wants to know the details of his death and where he is buried.

"She also mentioned an aunt Sinead and thought she was buried in Kerry, so Siobhan must have talked about her sister to her."

"As far as I'm aware the story she was told by her mother and Aunt Sally was that her aunt had been a victim of the troubles as was her dad, in a separate incident, and other than that and the story of how she came to be called Beibhinn were the only details of the past that she knew. Partly true and part fantasy, but I think the time for truth has come and I am dreading being the one to shatter her dreams."

Pearl looked over at him and could tell this guy really had Beibhinn's best interests at heart. She had grown up calling him uncle and to all intents and purposes he was the only family she had; she did not envy him the task that lay ahead.

"I will put off giving her any details if she calls in the next few days, but there will be details in the files of Sinead's past and demise, which we can pass on to her when you have given her the true facts of her life." She gave him a slip of paper. "These are my contact details, give me a ring and let me know how things are proceeding and I will tell the staff here to refer her to me if she comes in meantime."

They said their goodbyes and Pauric decided to call into Beibhinn's office and walk with her to the Scandia for lunch; he parked outside and was about to alight from the car when the door of the building opened and a ghost from his past walked by him.

He must be imagining things; that couldn't possibly be Ruth. His imagination was running riot. She had been in his mind so much since coming back to Belfast and now he was starting to hallucinate. *Get a grip Dub! You'll be going to the funny farm if you go on like this.*

Then Beibhinn came out of the door and smiled when she spotted him. "It's such a lovely day shall we walk to the Scandia? I feel the need for some air; it's been a bit of a hectic day."

"Of course, pet, my scheduled meeting was over early so I decided to meet you here. By the way, there was a middle aged lady who left the building just ahead of you, her face was familiar but maybe she is a doppelganger of a friend I used to know?"

"Oh, that would have been my friend and personnel officer Mary. I told you about her over the weekend. Lovely lady. I'd be lost without her," smiled Beibhinn. "Trust you to notice a pretty face, uncle Dub. Life in the old boy yet," she teased.

Mary, thought Pauric. *I must have been mistaken.*

Chapter 18

HUGHIE DEVLIN SET A HALF pint glass of cider down on the makeshift table in front of Johnny Rogers, saying, "Get that down ye, and watch out for the Peelers with their breathalysers on your way home," before he took a fit of coughing.

"How long have we been friends now, Hughie?" Johnny asked as he took a sip of the amber liquid, "And you think I give a fuck for Peelers, stuff them and all who sail with them."

"Easy on now, Johnny, my son's wee wife works with them and she's glad of the job and the money! You a loyal Prod and me a Provo and I'm standing up for the bastards and you're running them down, what is this world coming to?"

The two friends sipped on their drinks and started reminiscing about their weird friendship. For over twenty-five years they had known each other, ever since the days of Corrymeela and the cross community get- together and dances.

"Here, Johnny, do you remember the night our lot and yours got together at the community centre on the Shore Road? I think that was the first night I met you and the first time I saw that Brit Major. Boy, he was the cause of a lot of our squad getting in to so much strife! We should have finished him off when we had the chance but that Murphy whore spilled the beans and wrecked the whole operation."

"What Murphy bitch was that? Are you talking about Siobhan, the community relations girl? I saw her double the other day you know, had to do a double take, then realised it was too young to be her."

"Aye, wee Sinead's sister. If you saw her you were seeing a ghost, sure she was taken out a while ago, long runs the fox, but we got her in the end!"

"I liked those girls; do you remember 'Scotch Egg'? I could have had her you know; only the Major put his nose in!"

"In your dreams, Johnny. They thought they were better than the likes of us. They preferred fraternising with the Brits. A wee bit of tar and feathering would have been good fun and some of our women would have relished doing the deed, but it wasn't to be. As I said, all our plans were scuppered by that bitch Siobhan."

"Were you involved in that kidnapping and bust up with the pigs? I can vaguely remember it, but my memory isn't what it used to be. Was Major Phil not wiped out? I thought there was talk at the time that he was - and wasn't his death in the Belfast Telegraph?"

"I was a very minor part of it and lucky to escape and to this day very few know that I was involved. Most of that clique is dead now, but a few are still living in the past and working out of Dundalk. Good luck to them. I've had enough of trouble. This baccy business is safer for both of us, eh Johnny?"

He gave Johnny a clap on the back and went over to the rear of the industrial unit. Least said about his involvement that evening the better.

"You boys nearly finished? I want those seats put back properly and the car left in pristine condition," he said to the two youths working inside a Mitsubishi Space Wagon. "Have you put the parcels in my car?"

"Yes, Mr Devlin, all transferred. Will you need us again next week?"

"I'll be in touch when I need you again," he said, pulling two fifty pound notes from his back pocket and handing it to them. "Now on your way and be like Dad." They looked at him puzzled. "Keep Mum, you stupid fuckers!"

He turned round to where Johnny Rogers was still sitting nursing his glass." You want a fill up, mate?"

"No, no. I'll be on my way, Hughie. I was just thinking on our past dealings and we've had some quare times." He laughed. "By the way, I couldn't get hold of any rolling baccy this time but our contact says they should have more for us in about ten days. Will you do the next run or shall I?"

"Sure we can arrange that nearer the time. Are your lads doing the Nutts Corner Sunday Market this week or the Sunday car boot sale at Windsor Park? I have some guys covering Jonesborough, but don't want to step on your territory if it can be helped."

Johnny scratched his head. "Surely this is your week for

Nutts Corner; we do the third and fourth Sundays of the month?"

"This getting old is no fun Johnny, but look at us. Who would believe we are business partners?"

"…and doing not too badly, eh Hughie. Well we need to take care of our pensions, yes indeed who would believe it? I'd better be getting home and hope I don't see any more ghosts from the past."

Hughie opened the double doors and guided him out of the unit and waved him goodbye. *This guy I trust better than some of my own sort,* he thought as he tidied up, turned out the lights and locked the doors.

His task now was to pass on some of this pluck to his agents around the markets, no questions asked and no trail to follow, all strictly cash transactions; anyone caught took their own consequences.

He had one parcel on his front passenger seat and he pulled into a lay-by where an ice cream van was parked. A guy walked over to him and slipped notes into his hand before receiving the parcel. Hughie then continued with his journey to west Belfast, stopping at a chippie for a wee fish supper. *Nice way to end a lucrative day,* he thought.

Johnny's mind was working overtime on his way home. He knew Hughie had been mixed up in some rum goings on during the troubles as he had himself. They had both been guests of Her Majesty on a few occasions, and had always kept in contact, unknown to their respective companions. However, he didn't think his friend had been too involved, more on the prefatory like himself, but the incident he mentioned tonight was serious stuff, including the deaths of some of Hughie's team. Surely he hadn't blood on his hands?

He always thought why they got on so well. Was that because they were both minor tea leafs and, troubles or no troubles, still would have been on the make for a few bob, like-minded beings with a hard persona on the outside, but pussy cats within?

He didn't think he could have pulled a trigger on anyone. Yes, perhaps roughed them up a bit, but to kill? No way! He was a coward, but no one would ever guess how his stomach churned at the thought of killing.

As for seeing ghosts, that girl on the ferry from Scotland could have been Siobhan, albeit as she was twenty-five years ago. Could she possibly be a relative?

Enough rambling, Johnny Rogers! Think I'll treat the missus to a fish supper, he thought as he pulled into the Golden Fry on the Shore road.

Yes, the two friends did think alike, like two peas in a pod, be it on either side of the divide; they must have been separated at birth.

Chapter 19

DETECTIVE INSPECTOR McALISTER HAD worked over the weekend, checking and rechecking on names from the past who could possibly be dangerous to Beibhinn now.

Of all the known names, very few had survived and those who had were scattered around the world and as far as she could ascertain might possibly have died as well, either naturally or from foul deeds.

As there were some questions about a few of them, she decided it would be wiser for Pauric to stay put in Belfast until she could tell him it was safe to leave Beibhinn. This would pan out a lot easier, she thought, if Beibhinn were aware of all the circumstances, but who was she to offer advice? Pauric and Brian must surely have discussed bringing the girl up-to-date with her heritage, if not for her sake and safety, then for their consciences'? *Men,* she thought. *Can't live with them and we'd be lost without them.*

She thought back to her own short but eventful marriage to a former colleague. Never again, she vowed. If she was ever to marry again - and there was little chance of that - it would be to someone not in the force.

She and Bob had a blissful courtship and had made great plans for their future, a ten-year plan for promotion and then early retirement and emigration to Australia.

They had enjoyed a four-week honeymoon there, touring in a Volkswagen camper van and really seeing the country. They fell in love with the life style and made the decision to make this their home one day in the future. Unfortunately, that was never to be.

Bob was a victim of a bomb attack in the border area six short months into their marriage, and Pearl dealt had with her grief by concentrating on her career and living for the force and hoping peace would come sooner rather than later.

Now she was District Inspector and with retirement looming after thirty years' service she was determined to go quietly and not with a bang, which was why she wanted to make sure nothing was going to happen to Beibhinn. Well, not on her shift!

When Pauric telephoned her on Tuesday morning she told him of her fears. Until she could be sure none of the dissidents operating now were connected to Siobhan's history, well as sure as she could be, she thought it would be wise if he were to stay on in Belfast.

Her contacts were thin on the ground now, since the peace process; it was amazing how many touts had disappeared!

Pauric listened to her wise council and agreed to stay for a few more days - in fact Beibhinn had asked him to accompany her to Scotland on Thursday evening for a long week end and he thought now that might be the best solution; he knew Brian was still there and that could give them the best opportunity to tell all to Beibhinn in the company of her best friends.

Yes, he decided a trip to Scotland would be the best solution and a safer one, so he proceeded to telephone Brian at Glenside and they agreed Beibhinn should know everything and the sooner the better.

As they were having dinner that evening Pauric told Beibhinn he would be delighted to go to Scotland with her at the weekend and the smile on her face let him know that this was going to be the proper decision; he wanted her to keep on smiling and not let ghosts from the past spoil her life.

"That is great, uncle Dub. I'm so pleased you will be here tomorrow. I have asked Mary to join me for dinner. She has been so helpful since I arrived. I just want to show my appreciation and I really want you to meet her; she is a lovely woman."

"Sounds good, pet, but I hope you're not thinking of matchmaking? You know, I am a confirmed bachelor!"

Beibhinn laughed and gave him a hug, saying, "I had better phone and book a table for three then."

Chapter 20

BARRY DEVLIN SAT ON THE back porch of his semi and puffed slowly on his pipe. It was a glorious autumn evening and, looking around his well-tended garden with the leaves starting to turn golden, he felt at peace with the world. Who would have thought six months ago that he would be sitting here tonight as master of all he surveyed?

New house, new job and his darling wife in a new position too thanks to Joanne, his father's old friend warning her beforehand that vacancies were about to be advertised for clerical officers in the police authority. She had her CV prepared well in advance and referees willing to give her excellent references and now she was a civil servant with all the benefits to go with the position.

After graduating with a degree in accountancy. he had applied for so many positions in and around Belfast and was about to give up and go back to bar tending, a job that had seen him through university, along with a lot of financial help from his father, when out of the blue an international firm of accountants and financial advisers had started recruiting for their new Belfast office.

He felt his prayers had been answered when he had a successful interview and the offer of a job. It was as though his birthday and Christmas had come at the same time.

Then the house they had both dreamed of owning was within their reach as the occupants were emigrating and needed a quick sale. At last, they were property owners and moved in within three weeks; he still had to pinch himself to make sure it was not all a dream.

His father was sorry to see them move out of his home, of course, as he had enjoyed the company; it wasn't much fun living alone when getting on in life, but he wished them well in their new adventure.

Yes, Hughie would have to get used to living alone again. Since his darling wife had died he had felt the pangs of loneliness that she must have felt when he was off gadding about saving Ireland, as she called it!

Having Barry and Lisa live with him since they got married was a godsend, and stopped him from going insane. His past life, with all its gory details, was catching up with him now, and his health was deteriorating. He thought of the many nights he had spent in the fields around the border in County Armagh and holed up in remote farm houses and shivered at the thoughts.

He tried not to think of some of the things he had got up to with his comrades; those thoughts were the makings of nightmares, and now that he was alone again they were recurring.

Lisa interrupted Barry's musing, saying, "You haven't let on to your Da that this party on Wednesday night is for him? Does he still think it's a house warming?"

"What do you take me for? An eejit? I want this to be a night to remember for my da; one that I can say thank you for all the sacrifices he and Mum, God rest her soul, made for me. I know he's only sixty, Lisa, but he hasn't half aged in the last few years; I've only noticed how much since we have moved out."

"That's because you don't see him every day, so you're bound to see a difference in him, but enough of this small talk. Have you the drinks ordered for Wednesday? I have the food all in hand. Now, can you think of any of his friends we have forgotten, we don't seem to have a lot of people coming."

"Well, other than Joanne, I can't think of any other friends. Come to think of it, even when growing up there were never friends of his in our house. I think he was a bit of a loner and his job took him away for weeks on end, so he probably never really had time for friendships. Uncle Jim and Aunt Betty are coming and Cousin Monica and her new fella, so that will be eight, more than enough for our first house party," he said before knocking his pipe out on his heel and going back indoors. "I think I'll call up to see him tonight just for a wee chat and make sure he hasn't forgotten about tomorrow night; it wouldn't do if the guest of honour forgot to turn up, now would it? Do you want to come along with me? You know he loves to see you."

"Ok. As I said, I have all organised and a wee breath of air won't do us any harm and I am fond of your da."

Hughie was pleased to see them. "Would you like a wee cuppa tea?" he asked as they sat down.

"You just sit there and talk to Barry. I'll do the honours while you chat," said Lisa, making her way into the kitchen.

"How's work going, son? Are you settling in ok?" asked Hughie.

"Sure am," said Barry as he fumbled in his inside coat pocket and pulled out a photograph. "This is the team I am working with; we were all at the Duke of York last week on a 'bonding' session," he explained before he passed the photo to Hughie.

Hughie thought his heart had stopped, then started pounding again so fast that he was sure it could be noticed through his shirt. He hesitated and looked again, yes it was her and now he knew who Johnny had seen on the boat from Scotland! No mistaking that must be a relative of Siobhan's.

"Who are the two ladies at each end?" he asked as Lisa came into the room with the tea tray.

"The one on the right is Mary Porter, personnel officer, and on the left, Beibhinn Sweeney, recruitment officer on secondment from head office."

"Let's have a look," said Lisa as she sat the tray down on the coffee table. "Oh, I've seen that girl before," she said pointing to Beibhinn. "She came into enquiries the other day looking for some information on her father and aunt. I think D.I. McAlister is dealing with her."

"Beibhinn, son of Brian," mused Hughie.

"Pardon, Da?"

"An old Irish name son, meaning son of Brian, from the days of Brian Boru. So, what are these two like? Easy to work with?"

"The best, Da. In fact, the whole team is great. I just love going in every day, and on that note," he said finishing off his tea, "we better make tracks if we don't want to over sleep in the morning. Pick you up at seven tomorrow night, Da?"

"That's great, son. I look forward to celebrating your new home and may you have a very happy life there."

On the way home Barry keep worrying about his father. "Do you think my da is going senile, Lisa?"

"Whatever do you mean, love?"

"You don't remember him when he was younger, but there was a hardness then which has disappeared."

"Are you trying to say your da's growing soft in his oul age?" she laughed. "He's not that old, he's only turning sixty."

"Alright love, perhaps he's just mellowing with age, and he really seemed interested in my work colleagues, now that's a first. He was never ever interested in any of my friends at Uni, not that I had many."

"You talking to yourself, Barry Devlin? Now, that's the first sign of losing your marbles and you have the cheek to blame your da! Let's have an early night and christen the spare room."

"Lisa Devlin! Whatever happened to the shy wee girl I married?"

"I think she got turned on by the shy wee lad she married," she giggled as they garaged the car and went indoors.

Chapter 21

"WHO WAS ON THE 'PHONE, darling?" asked Lisa, rubbing her hair briskly with a towel. She tightened her robe around her and proceeded to the kitchen.

"It was Bridie, just letting us know she was able to get a baby sitter for tonight so she and Liam will be joining us for the celebrations," replied Barry. He smiled and put his arms around Lisa, nuzzling into her neck. "That won't be a problem, will it?" he questioned.

"No problem. Catering wise, we have enough here to feed the proverbial five thousand, but much as I like Bridie I just can't stand Liam, there's something creepy about him and I just can't put my finger on what it is," Lisa replied.

"Well, he is one of me da's friends, Lisa. As much as we

may dislike him it's only for a few hours and if it keeps Dad happy having friends here, sure that makes it all worthwhile, and he can't be all bad or why would Bridie have put up with him all these years?"

"Maybe having four kids has a lot to do with that," she replied, "but as you say it's only for a few hours - and look what I found in the spare room," she said holding up a photo frame. "Your works photo would be nice in this."

"That's perfect," he said, taking the frame from her. "Now, I better be getting off to work or it will be my ex works photo I'll be displaying. Do you need a lift?"

"No, it's ok. I have today off. Joanne adjusted the rota. I'm off today and tomorrow but will cover for her on Saturday, so I have all day to prepare and make myself beautiful for you," she said, laughing.

"Are you sure a day would be enough," he jested as he ran out through the door laughing and she flung the damp towel after him.

"Cheeky bugger!" she shouted after him. "I'll make you pay for that remark."

"Promises, promises," was heard at a distance from the garage.

That evening Barry picked his father up from his home and drove the short distance to his new house. It was amazing how well they got on together now as it hadn't always been the case when he was growing up and witnessing the hardships his mother went through when Hughie spent time in her Majesty's establishments or off on another mission. Yes, they were hard times and it was so good now they were all behind them and people could start living in peace. He never could see the sense in fighting over a bit of land and had to keep his ideologies to himself when at Queen's University on his da's advice. Better to be a 'nerd' than a' reactionary', he had been told, and possibly a dead reactionary.

No, politics and religion were two subjects he steered clear off and that was another reason he disliked Liam; a few drinks in him and all sense left him. His party songs left a lot to be desired and could cause offence in mixed circles; luckily no one was among the guest list tonight to be offended, and everyone knew Liam's form and usually ignored it.

He checked his watch: seven forty-five. Everyone should be in place for the surprise welcome for Hughie.

"I didn't get out to get you a house warming present, son," said Hughie as Barry pulled into the driveway. "But here you are - this is for you and wee Lisa and you can buy whatever you need for your new home," he said, pulling a wad of notes from his top pocket and placing them in Barry's hand.

Barry looked at the money, and said, "Da there is far too much here and you're on benefits and can't afford this."

Hughie tapped his nose, and replied, "From my rainy day fund, son, and sure don't we get a lot of them in this wee land. Now no nonsense, put that away safely and give it to Lisa after the housewarming."

There was no arguing with Hughie when he had made his mind up, so Barry complied and put the money in his back pocket.

"You're a terrible man, Da. Thank you so much, this is very much appreciated, if you weren't such a man's man I'd give you a hug."

"Don't you dare, son! Think what that would do for my

reputation," he laughed. "Big Hughie giving out hugs, wily nily. God, I'd never live that down!"

He silently wiped a tear from his cheek as he alighted from the car. Barry opened the door and stood aside, allowing Hughie to enter first, to be greeted by the surprise gathering.

He stood for a moment in amazement as the crowd in front of him sang Happy Birthday. He just couldn't believe his eyes; all his family and what friends he had left, here to wish him Happy Birthday. *Perhaps there is a God, and he is starting to forgive me. Thank you, Lord*, he silently whispered.

"God almighty, you lot kept this quiet," he stammered as he accepted the glass from someone's hand, "and you're here too, Liam. Have you nothing better to do?" he laughed.

Liam nodded for him to come closer. "Have you seen that photo on the sideboard, Hughie?" he whispered.

"I've only just arrived, you big eejit! I haven't even seen the sideboard, never mind a photo," he said as he walked after Liam across the room.

Everyone was chatting and catching up, so the two friends looking at a photo went unnoticed.

"Look, who's in that photo with your Barry."

Now Hughie knew what he was talking about; it was only a matter of time for someone to notice. Unfortunately it had to be Liam.

"Yes, they're our Barry's work colleagues and that's the end of it, savvy!"

Liam stepped back at the tone of Hughie's voice, more like the Hughie of old when he was commander than the old man he had become of late. Bridie joined them and picked up the photo.

"Oh my God, Liam. Look, there's that girl I told you about," he declared, pointing to Beibhinn in the photograph.

"What girl? Sure you ramble on all the time and never give my head peace," he spluttered, spilling some of his drink on the carpet.

Hughie tried to defuse the situation; he didn't like a drunken Liam. Drink could loosen his tongue and he didn't want that to happen here. "Barry, do you have a cloth to mop this up before it stains your carpet, and don't give this eejit any more alcohol."

"As I was saying," continued Bridie, "that girl is the one who slipped me the twenty pound note in the Bodega just before I had the child; you must remember Liam. Didn't you take it off me and blow it all on drink! She was a lovely girl. Not many like her in a dozen."

"Hughie," whispered Liam as Bridie helped with cleaning up his mess, "is she anything to the grass Siobhan? And did you notice who else is in the photo?"

Hughie gripped his upper arm so hard he winced. "You didn't see a photo in here and if you did you didn't know anyone in it, OK? Do you understand or shall I spell it out for you, you miserable piece of shit?"

He let go of Liam's arm and left him trying to get the circulation going again and went to speak to his other guests. He was going to enjoy this birthday party and he had plenty of time later to decide what was to be done.

Chapter 22

BEIBHINN WAS REALLY LOOKING FORWARD to dinner this evening and introducing Mary to uncle Dub. She just knew they would get on well together. They had the same sense of humour and were of the same age bracket, so why should they not get along?

Mary had suggested eating out of town and perhaps in her neck of the woods, Holywood in County Down. So Beibhinn had complied and booked the table for three in The Dirty Duck, an alehouse and restaurant well known and highly recommended by anyone she had mentioned it to. It sat on the shores of Belfast Lough with wonderful panoramic views. She hoped this would be a wonderful evening she so loved having uncle Dub here, felt like she was part of a family again.

While Beibhinn was at the office Pauric called Pearl to see

if there had been any developments. She was worried to hear there were at least two old hands from the 70's who would possibly remember Siobhan and spot the likeness to her daughter Beibhinn.

One was a Hugh Devlin whom she didn't think would be a problem as he had health issues and mainly house bound. The other was a Liam Gray who could be a bit of a loose cannon; apparently an alcoholic who had spent more time in Crumlin Road Prison in Belfast on thieving charges than he had ever spent in the Maze Jail on terrorist charges.

Armed with this knowledge made Pauric all the more determined to get Beibhinn safely to the mainland and possibly back to Tasmania as soon as possible. He had chatted with Brian who was still with Sarah and Angus and he agreed, Beibhinn's safety was paramount and the sooner she knew all the facts the better.

Pauric offered to drive to Holywood as he wasn't a drinker and Beibhinn could enjoy a little vino and relax this evening. She had worked non- stop since coming to the province; in fact, she was a bit of a workaholic and would have to learn how to relax, he thought.

The journey from Belfast to Holywood had changed quite a bit since he was last here all those years ago when he had driven the route so many times for meetings in Palace Barracks with Brian, Phil, Harry and Joe. He turned off the main road onto Kinnegar Road overlooking the beach and parked as close to the establishment as possible.

He helped Beibhinn from the car and offered her his arm.

"Hold on to me in case you fall off those heels," he laughed, looking at her four inch stilettos.

She playfully slapped his arm, saying, "When I get to your age I'll take help walking, but for now I'm fine." She gave a little dance, showing him how able she was to walk in the heels.

"You're as daft as a brush," he quipped, laughing as he followed her into reception.

"I have a table for three booked, the name's Sweeney," she told the young waiter who approached them. "My friend hasn't arrived yet so we will wait in the bar if that's ok. We are a little early."

"That's fine, Mam. I'll send your friend in to the bar when she arrives, what is the name?"

"Porter, Mary Porter," she replied, smiling as she walked into the bar.

Pauric had already ordered her a martini aperitif and a non-alcoholic beer for himself, when she sat down.

"This is very comfortable and cosy," he said to her. "Cheers, and here's to everything you wish for yourself in the future my dear." They clinked glasses.

"Very profound, uncle Dub, and slainte to you."

Pauric was sitting with his back to the doorway when Mary arrived. Beibhinn stood up and waved to her friend as she came through the door.

"Over here, Mary," she beckoned.

Pauric stood up and turned around to greet Beibhinn's friend, smiling, but the smile froze as he came face to face with Ruth Yorke.

"Ruth," he stammered. "Is it really you?" Before she realised what was happening he had her in his arms. "I never ever thought I would ever see you again"

Beibhinn was very puzzled.

"Uncle Dub, this is my friend Mary, Mary Porter," she said hesitantly and confused.

"She was also my friend, Beibhinn, Ruth Yorke," he explained, smiling down at Ruth. "We knew each other long before you were born, in another time and another place, a lifetime ago."

Ruth was speechless. She sat down and lifted Beibhinn's drink and took a gulp, coughed and spluttered, "What is this? I think it's a wee Black Bush I need - in fact a double Black Bush. Oh my good God, my heart will never last out to any more shocks. So now I'm Mary and you are Dub? Whatever happened to Pauric?"

Beibhinn looked on in amazement. It was as though a play was enfolding in front of her, and the main actors were her uncle Dub and her friend Mary, and she was the only one in the audience.

So she thought.

Chapter 23

THE WAITER INTERRUPTED THE explanations by informing the group their table was ready and as they rose to go into the dining area Pauric was able to whisper to Ruth, "She knows nothing of the past."

Ruth's mind was working overtime. Obviously Beibhinn was completely in the dark about her family's history, or else why should she be spending all her time looking for, what now turns out to be, a fictitious father? As the pieces of the jigsaw in her mind started falling into place she realised why Beibhinn had seemed so familiar to her; she could be a clone of her mother. Why hadn't this occurred to her before?

She decided to let Pauric do any explanation required and follow his lead, until she could talk to him without Beibhinn being present. That would be the best policy.

"Ruth, why are you now Mary?" asked Pauric as they waited between courses.

"Well, I was always Mary Ruth," she smiled. "My cousins in Dublin always gave me my full title but over the years I abbreviated it to Mary, less pompousness, don't you think? And you, why Dub?"

Dub looked at her and marvelled at how good the years had been to her, she was still the girl he had fallen in love with and by the way his heart was feeling, it still remembered her with love.

"When I settled in Tasmania and took up my position in the radio station the guys there christened me Dub because of my Irish accent and the name kind of stuck. Some of them don't even remember I was once called Pauric." He laughed at this thought. "… and with starting a new life," he continued, "it was apt that I should forget the old and try to get on with things."

He looked at her with such intensity she knew exactly what he meant. Hadn't she done exactly the same and tried to forget her past life?

After her spell in the mental institution she moved to Liverpool and enrolled in John Moore's university where she sat for her masters. Changing her name to Porter, her mother's maiden name, gave her a new beginning and she had forgotten her past as Ruth Yorke to all intents and purposes, until now.

"So is there a Mr Porter?" he asked, wishing he could retract the question almost immediately.

"No, no," she spluttered. "I sat my masters under that name and it sort of helped with my transformation into a 'new me', so Mary Porter I have remained."

Beibhinn was fascinated by the conversation between these

two friends and somehow felt there had been a lot more going on between them than either were owning up to at the moment.

How intriguing, she thought, her mind starting to work overtime. *Was this the love of his life of which there had been rumours about at the station? And why had it ended, if so?*

She would question him further when they had their trip to Scotland, she decided, and not embarrass the two friends here by prying.

In the bar Liam Gray ordered another beer and couldn't believe his luck - Ruth Yorke in the company of the Siobhan look-a-like. What a feather in his cap if he could work something out to make him rise in the estimation of his comrades.

He had to think carefully and draw up a plan to maybe finish off the job Terry had gone to Australia to do. He knew Terry had given the tout Siobhan her comeuppance but lost his own life in completing the deed. What if he finished off the bastard? How good would this make him look among his mates?

Thinking of it gave him a weird sense of pleasure, but then how many of his mates remembered the happenings of the Seventies? His befuddled mind was in a state of confusion.

Terry had gone solo to Australia on a self-styled mission, not one that had been authorised by their group, so how would they react if he went on a solo mission to eradicate anything left on this earth belonging to Miss Murphy? Would it give him better standing in the organisation or punishment for bringing attention to them?

He would have a discreet word with Bridie when he got home. Her brain was clear and she had kept him on the straight and narrow on more than one occasion.

She was a true Republican, so surely she would approve of this plan to rid Ireland of touts and all belonging to them? With her blessing and help he could work out something that was foolproof.

Sure, hadn't she had sat up with him all night after he had heard that his mate Terry had drowned, Terry who had always treated him with respect.

Yes, he would relish finishing what they started all those years ago. It may not be an Army Major, but she was the daughter of a tout who would meet her maker at his hand.

The thought made him glow. His pickled brain was in a feeble state and trying to use it could prove dangerous. He could pick this little lady up at any time now that he knew where she worked, thanks to Barry's photo of his work mates. The plan's a good one, he thought, as he finished his beer and ordered another one.

The get-together and dinner was proving to be a very nostalgic night for Dub and Mary. They talked about places and people that would have no significance to Beibhinn. Mary had gathered Beibhinn was completely in the dark about her mother's past, and it was not her place to enlighten her. Poor girl, she had so much to learn.

As the night came to a close and contact details had been exchanged, Beibhinn and Dub took off for their journey back to Belfast. Beibhinn was looking forward to introducing uncle Dub to her friends in Scotland tomorrow. *What a great weekend this is going to be,* she thought, *all my favourite people together and just think if Philip hadn't been such a prick he would have been there too, his loss, not mine.*

Chapter 24

YOU ARE THINKING OF DOING what? You bloody eejit! Who the fuck do you think you are, Ireland's answer to Che Guevara? In fact, you are incapable of thinking! My ma was right; I never should have married you. She said I would have picked better in a lucky dip, and she wasn't far wrong!"

Bridie was seething; she couldn't believe what this excuse for a husband of hers was planning, and there was no use arguing with him now, he was too intoxicated to comprehend.

Oh good God above, what am I to do?

She reckoned Hughie would know how to deal with this. He was one of the few 'friends' from Liam's past who still kept in touch and looked out for him, knowing the booze over the years was affecting his brain.

That wee girl, a total stranger, had reached out to her with compassion and this hateful scum, she happened to be married to, wanted to kidnap and kill her.

This can't be happening, this is a nightmare!

She vowed to get in touch with Hughie tomorrow to sort it out once and for all. She didn't want her four kids growing up in this atmosphere; peace had come after all the years of the troubles, and that was what she wanted for her kids, peace!

She had arranged for her sister to come to stay overnight next week. Before then, she had booked into the local clinic to be sterilised - no more wee babies; she had had enough!

Hughie Devlin listened intently as Bridie explained what Liam was planning to do. She had taken the day off work to come visit him and left the kids at their normal day care, even though she could not afford to lose the wages, but needs must, and this had to be sorted.

Hughie assured her he would have words with Liam over the week end. He was expecting to meet up with Johnny on Monday to arrange delivery of another shipment of tobacco and share the payment for the last consignment.

He saw her on her way and told her not to worry, that he would sort everything out, by Monday at the latest. She breathed a sigh of relief when Hughie gave his word - things would be sorted, he'd said, and she trusted him.

After Bridie had left, Hughie thought what a morning this had been. It had been confirmed he had cancer of the pancreas and his GP, who had called to see him before Bridie had arrived, had told him to put his house in order, that nothing could be done for him other than pain relief.

He already had a will made, leaving everything he possessed to Barry and giving him power of attorney if he became unable to handle his own affairs, but from what the doctor had told him there would not be a prolonged state of deterioration, so this would not be necessary.

He thought back over his life as he prepared to meet his maker. *Funny how the past can return to bite you on the arse,* he thought.

He remembered the night well when he had beaten Major Phil to a pulp and knew he would have had no hesitation in finishing him off, all for Ireland! And promising a very young Liam the first 'turn' with 'Scotch Egg', as Johnny had called her, when she was brought to the remote cottage.

He still talked of his disappointment at not 'sampling' her, even to this day! Poor Bridie, shackled to that waste of space, something he knew full well he could resolve. Yes, he had a lot of loose ends to tidy up and no better man for the job. This had given him a purpose to do some good in this very bad life he had lived.

He knew one good deed would not wipe out all the bad, but at least it would go some way to showing how he regretted his past.

Scotland

Pauric was welcomed with open arms into their home by Sarah and Angus, although she had never met or worked with him in the past. Over the last few days Brian had been telling her and Angus how they had all worked together and how good a team they were. When he related how it was a tip-off from him through a contact that had scuppered the assault and intended killing of Phil and her abduction, she knew she owed her life to him.

After the introductions, Beibhinn left uncle Dub with his friends, Brian, Angus and Sarah, to go over to Caitlin's and Steven's house next door, for a very welcome catch up. She had so much to tell them and was still in a state of excitement at having uncle Dub here too; she knew her friends would love him as much as she did.

After she left, it was discussed how and when to tell her the whole truth about her past. Sarah felt it might be better coming primarily from Brian and then she could confirm the happenings before her mother was whisked off to the other side of the world, and Pauric could fill in all the details from there.

They decided it would be better to leave this until after dinner when all the family and friends would gather in Glenside. Sarah thought Beibhinn would cope better with her best friend, Caitlin, by her side.

Caitlin and Steven had been told all the details before Beibhinn had arrived and they also completely agreed; the sooner she learnt the truth the better.

In fact, Steven had wanted to get in touch with Philip and explain the situation and ask him to come to Glenside and support Beibhinn. Sarah had dissuaded him.

"I know being twins you want to look out for your brother Steven, but this, in Beibhinn's eyes, could be a step too far and be actually viewed as interference in their affairs. Beibhinn has made it perfectly clear she and Philip are no more, as a couple, and we have to respect that decision. If at some stage they do get back together, well at least we won't be accused of taking sides or sticking our noses where they are not wanted."

"You are right, Sarah," said Steven, "someday I hope I have

your wisdom. Better leave well alone, I suppose, and see how things pan out."

"You are a very caring man, Steven, and I admire how close you are to Philip. I couldn't have wished for a better husband for my daughter."

Sarah left the men to chat as she went to the kitchen to give Annie a hand at preparing lunch and then deciding between them what to have for dinner that evening. She really did have to keep busy.

She wished it was tomorrow and everything was out in the open. Too many secrets had been kept over the years, but now was the time for closure and a safe future for them all.

Just as she was about to pour a welcome cup of coffee for herself and Annie the kitchen door opened.

"Is there one in the pot for me?" asked a smiling Marcy. "I thought I would come up and surprise Stewarty. This is the longest we have been apart since getting together and I thought he would relish some support when talking to Beibhinn."

Sarah gave her friend a hug, saying "Always one in the pot for you, and so glad you could make it. Is all the selling finished? Have you finally laid your empire to rest?"

"Last one signed on the dotted line yesterday, now I am no longer a 'business woman', just a lady of leisure. I'd better let Stewarty know I've arrived," she said as she grabbed her mug of hot coffee and went to join the men in the lounge.

"That's our Marcy," said Sarah to Annie. "Always in a rush and on the go. I can't see her as a lady of leisure, by no stretch of the imagination."

Annie agreed.

Chapter 25

BEIBHINN THOUGHT SHE WAS HAVING a nightmare. Here she was in Glenside with all those she held dear, but being told her life, as she knew it, had all been a lie; she wanted to scream and perhaps wake up. This couldn't possibly be reality.

Oh please let this be a dream, she silently screamed. There was too much information to take on board. Every time anyone spoke, she was hearing more and when uncle Dub started explaining how her mother had died, that was just too much, and she collapsed in a heap on the floor.

When she came to she was in bed with Caitlin by her side. Caitlin was taking her pulse and smiled at her when she opened her eyes.

"How are you feeling now? My heart truly goes out to you,

Beibhinn. What a lot of information you had to ingest this evening. I'll give you a sedative and let you have a rest, we can talk tomorrow," she said, signalling to her friend not to speak. "Just rest now, you have had enough for one day." She handed two tablets to her friend and a glass of water. "Take these and try to sleep. It's what your poor overworked brain needs: some rest."

Beibhinn nodded to her and snuggled into the soft duvet. She was much too tired to argue. Perhaps when she awakened in the morning she would discover this had all been a horrible dream.

Caitlin sat down beside her and held her hand until she was in a deep sleep, then tiptoed out of the room and quietly closed the door behind her.

She returned to the lounge where everyone was waiting to see how Beibhinn was.

"She's in a deep sleep now and will be alright until tomorrow morning, so may I suggest we all retire now and be here for her when she wakens? Do you mind if I stay here tonight, Mum? And is that ok by you?" She directed that last question to Steven.

"Of course it's alright darling, poor Beibhinn. What a lot of information and she was so unsuspecting. I feel so guilty. Perhaps I should have said something to her when we chatted in the past about Siobhan, but then it is only recently we have all had it confirmed as to her heritage; I can only imagine what she is going through."

"Well, ladies if you want to retire for the night go ahead, but I think wee single malt wouldn't go astray for the gents," proffered Angus.

"Gents my arse, if you excuse the expletive," said Marcy. "I think after the pressure and cliff hanging confessions of this evening we all deserve a wee dram. What say you, Sarah?"

Sarah had to smile, the more she got to know Marcy she had come to realise the lady called a spade a spade; there was no beating around the bush with her, so who was she to argue.

Steven had morning surgery to cover, Saturday morning surgery being quite busy normally and he didn't expect his wife to work with him as Beibhinn was feeling so poorly, no, she would be needed here. He kissed her on the cheek and told her to call him if he was needed, then said his goodnights to everyone else. Caitlin followed suit when he had left and went to the room adjacent to Beibhinn's to be near if she was needed.

Brian felt shattered. He accepted the glass of amber liquid from Angus and took a gulp. He didn't know how Beibhinn had reacted to the news that he was her father; it was so surreal as he was speaking to her. She just looked at him in amazement, and then Sarah had taken over and told her how she had worked with her mother in the province and also with Phil, Brian and the rest of the team. Dub had concluded with the story of how Siobhan had come to Tasmania and of how and why she had been murdered.

No wonder the poor girl had passed out! Her life had just been torn apart. Dub didn't remember if anyone had said how worried they all were when she went to work in the Province. That could be rectified tomorrow, yes, tomorrow they would all have to answer any questions she may ask and he was sure there would be a lot.

Pauric sipped slowly at his drink. He hadn't got around to telling Beibhinn how Ruth - or Mary as she knew her - fitted in to the jig saw that was her life; he vowed there would be no more secrets, he would tell her all over the weekend, a little at a time. Thinking of Ruth, he must telephone her over the weekend. He didn't want to lose her again and hoped she felt the same.

Marcy for once was quiet. Her heart had gone out to Brian when he was explaining to Beibhinn how he was possibly her father. If she wanted proof Angus could arrange for a DNA test to be done.

Sarah held Angus's hand and felt so blessed having this strong man in her life. In a crisis he was the only one she wanted near her and he had been so masterful tonight, taking charge when Beibhinn had collapsed and making sure she was ok before leaving her with Caitlin in the bedroom. Perhaps if she had broached the subject of Siobhan in the past there would have been less information for the poor wee lassie to take in.

They finished their drinks and made their way to their rooms, hoping for some well-earned sleep to help them cope with whatever was to be thrown at them tomorrow.

Chapter 26

HUGHIE LOOKED AROUND HIS NEAT and tidy room. The care assistant had just left and he had had his strong medication which would keep him going for the next few hours; yes, he thought, as he placed an envelope, addressed to Barry, on the mantle shelf, everything neat and tidy, just the way life should be.

He had already telephoned Liam and told him to be here at two, sober and with his car. He had also arranged to meet Johnny at the lock-up to settle up the cash owing from the last consignment of tobacco.

There was very little to be done now and he smiled at the thought of how well organised he was. The adrenalin was rising, but in a good way, not in the way it used to be when they were out on a job - that was sickening, but this felt good.

Surprisingly Liam was on time and as relatively sober as an alcoholic could be. He looked excited.

"Are we going on a job, Hughie? Just like old times, you and me together, eh Hughie?"

Hughie laughed. There was something child-like about this man. Ravaged by booze and hatred over the years, he was still getting a kick out of the thought of evil; child-like, yes but a very wicked child!

"Just a wee job, Liam. I need you as a driver, just follow my directions and no wild driving, we don't want to draw attention to ourselves."

"The job's a good one," said Liam, tapping his nose. "Mum's the word. Do you need help out to the car?" he asked noticing Hughie lift a walking stick.

"There's life in this old dog yet," smiled Hughie. "The day I need help will never come."

They both went to the car and Hughie directed Liam across town to the lock-up where he had arranged to meet Johnny. They drove the car inside and Hughie told Johnny to wait outside and make sure he and his friend were not disturbed.

"Am I your personal guard today, Hughie?" drooled Liam.

"That's right, Liam. I'm having a very important meeting and can't be disturbed, so just keep your eyes peeled and let us know if anyone comes snooping about."

On his arrival, Johnny sat on one of the chairs and lit a cigarette. "Is he the full shilling, Hughie?" he asked. "Are you babysitting today?"

"Something like that, it keeps him out of harm's way! Let's get on with this, don't want him drawing attention to us, do we?"

When the two old friends had finished their business, Hughie told Liam to come inside and close the doors.

"Well, did I do a good job, boss?" he asked.

"The best, mate, just like old times. Now, here you are," he said handing over a stiff whiskey. "You've earned this today."

"Is it ok drinking this before I drive you home?"

"For fuck sake, Liam, when did having a drink ever stop you driving? Are you turning over a new leaf in your old age?"

Liam knocked it back in one go and smiled at Hughie. The smiled died on his face as he watched Hughie tighten the silencer on his old tried and trusted fire arm, the one he had retrieved from its secret hiding place this morning. Hughie knocked back his glass of drink, said a 'Hail Mary', then put the nozzle to Liam's head and pulled the trigger before turning the gun on himself.

Johnny had just turned his car onto the Shore road when he remembered he had not made plans with his old mate for the next shipment; they had been so busy sorting out the cash they hadn't decided who was to do the next run, although by the look of Hughie he didn't think he would be capable of doing many more runs.

Age and illness were taking their toll on both of them now, but they had loved this wee bit of excitement they had had over the last couple of years, since the ceasefire. Their wee business had been a very rewarding hobby and kept them both busy, he thought, and it was very lucrative, too!

He turned the car and headed back to the lock up. There was no sign of Hughie's wee side-kick. Perhaps they had already left, he reckoned. He drove up to the door and noticed the lock was not in place, not that there was anything to pinch in there; they used it more as a meeting place where they could exchange the spoils of their business rather than a storehouse.

I'd better check, he thought.

He opened the doors and couldn't believe what he was seeing. A stream of blood was meandering across the uneven floor from where two lifeless bodies lay. He ran back to his car and didn't stop driving until he got home. Luckily, his wife and her sister had gone into the town.

There was a bottle of Vat19 in the drinks globe. He poured a glass and downed it in one, then he had a cup of tea. He had to work out what to do.

If he went to the cops he would have to explain what he was doing there, but at the same time God knows when anyone else would discover them. He didn't want his mate to be lying there over the weekend. He had to do something.

Finally, he decided to drive across town and find a phone box, call the cops and report something strange going on at the lock-ups; that way he would not be involved.

That done, he headed back home to grieve for his most unlikely best friend.

Chapter 27

BEIBHINN AND PAURIC WALKED SIDE by side along the banks of the loch. They had so much to talk about and Sarah had recommended this place as the most tranquil and stress relieving place on earth; they had driven the few miles to Luss, parked the car and headed to the loch side.

The views were breath-taking and on this calm autumn morning the colours magnificent, from deep browns to yellows and heady reds, a feast for weary eyes. Brian had wanted to explain so much to Beibhinn but she wanted to have a chat with her uncle Dub first, which was quite understandable. He was the only one who had been there for her since her birth.

Dub tried to explain, without causing any more stress, how her mother had come to live her life in Tasmania. He reiterated it wasn't that she had no love for Brian, quite the opposite. She loved him so much that she disappeared from his life to ensure he had a good future doing the job he loved.

He explained she was completely unaware that she was pregnant when she undertook the great change in her life.

"On discovering this after being in Tasmania a few weeks she decided to make the best of life and built her world around you after you arrived."

Beibhinn smiled at this thought. Her mother was such an independent person and truly lived life to the full and Beibhinn had had a blessed life with Siobhan and Auntie Sally - and with Uncle Dub her family was complete.

Going through school she had never felt the absence of a father as Dub had always been her father figure, so she felt she had never been denied the feeling of family completeness.

Since meeting Brian, she had always thought well of him and was quite looking forward to having him and Marcy as in laws, but now, could she ever think of him as her father? Maybe this was going a step too far too soon.

"Now do you understand why we were all so worried when you decided to go and work in Northern Ireland, especially when you said you wanted to trace your roots?" said Dub as he stopped at a lochside bench and sat down.

Beibhinn picked up a few pebbles and sat down beside him. She skimmed them over the water and watched the ripples form into circles before disappearing. "Was I really in so much danger? Surely those from the past who had relentlessly hunted down my mother are no longer active, or maybe no longer alive?"

"Who's to know how far the knowledge of dissidents spreads? Or how much significance your appearance in the

Province would mean to them? We are aware of at least two members from the seventies who would have known Siobhan, and are still living in Belfast, albeit inactive, to all intents and purposes, for many years. So we didn't want to take any chances with your safety, you do understand that, don't you?"

"To be quite honest, uncle Dub, my understanding has gone to pot. I have just discovered my whole life has been a lie and until I get the truth firmly fixed in my brain I am not capable of understanding much at all."

Dub put his arm around her shoulders and gave her a hug and decided 'in for a penny in for a pound'.

"Are you ready for any more revelations, my dear? I want to be completely honest with you and never have any more secrets between us."

Beibhinn looked at him in amazement.

"You mean there's more? Oh my God in heaven! How much more can I take?"

"Nothing bad, darling, but I want everything out in the open."

He proceeded to tell her about Ruth, or Mary as Beibhinn knew her, and how she had played a big part in his life before moving to Tasmania and how he had never really gotten over her.

"Is that why you and Mum never got together?" interrupted Beibhinn.

"I suppose that was one of the reasons," he mused, "but Siobhan and I were such good friends we really didn't want to ruin a good friendship."

He smiled down at her and then continued to explain why they had parted and how she had saved Phil's life and probably

Sarah's as well. He shuddered at the thought of what could have happened to that lovely lady.

Beibhinn was quiet for some time as she tried to make sense of everything she had been told, and then the questions eventually came tumbling out.

"Was Mary never in danger? How come she can live in the Province if it's still dangerous? And has she known all along who I am? Is that why she has been so kind to me?"

"Whoa girl, one question at a time! Mary was not aware who you were until we met in Holywood, so she was kind to you because she was fond of you, nothing else, and she was never in any danger as no one knew about us, or that she had overheard the plans on that dastardly evening.

"Her brother, Terry, whom she broke off contact with after that episode, was the only person who knew she was involved with a Dubliner, but never guessed who I was or what my occupation was. Owing to her ending up in a local institution for mentally ill patients and then moving to Liverpool and out of his life, he was hell bent on revenge."

"So that was the reason he hunted my mother down and murdered her?"

"Yes, in a nutshell. In his twisted mind Siobhan had been the cause of Ruth being brought to the Castlereagh Holding Centre for questioning by police and therefore the cause of her mental breakdown. For all of her life she had been his little sister doing everything she was told and looking after him like a mother - that was the reason she visited her cousins in Dublin once a month, to get a break from him and his bullying ways. So in some ways I have him to thank for her coming into my life."

"Do you want her back in your life?" Beibhinn asked.

"Well, we shall just have to see, my little matchmaker," he smiled at her glad to see a light in her eyes.

"All being well, I really would want to go back and finish the job I was sent to do Dub," admitted Beibhinn. "We only have the first batch recruited and started training, but I reckon the way things are progressing, six months should complete our quota and then I will approach my bosses for a transfer back home. That was what I had intended doing before all these revelations and I don't see any reason to change my mind."

Dub agreed that if the powers that be could guarantee her safety there should be no reason why she shouldn't fulfil her plans but meantime she should request a week's holiday leave until things became clearer.

"You are so clever, uncle Dub. What would I do without you?"

They rose in unison and slowly walked back to where they had left the car, savouring the breath-taking scenery as they walked.

"This really is a magical place, Dub."

He agreed.

When they arrived back at Glenside Brian was on the lawn smoking a cigarette. Marcy did not approve of this 'filthy habit', as she called it, and he was trying to give it up, but today he needed the calming weed.

Beibhinn went inside to join the other ladies having a coffee in the kitchen, while outside, Angus was pulling some unwanted weeds from the flower beds.

Dub, meanwhile, found Brian sitting on a garden seat and he joined him.

"Pearl McAlister was on the phone wanting to talk to you," said Brian. "I told her you would return the call when you got back. She said it wasn't urgent. Do you know I haven't spoken to that girl or woman as she is now, since she brought me the 'dear John' note from Siobhan?"

"She's an inspector now," said Dub. "She has done rather well for herself and hasn't changed a bit as far as looks go. I'll maybe go and return her call now; she may have some updates on how safe it is for Beibhinn to be here. I have convinced Beibhinn to stay for another week until we get some more information and it will also give you a chance to be more acquainted as father and daughter."

Brian put his cigarette out as his friend went into Glenside. He was looking forward to having a private talk with Beibhinn and he hoped, too, that Marcy would accept that past was the past and that's where it would stay.

Yes, he had loved Siobhan with a passion, but that was over twenty years ago and a distant memory until Beibhinn had been outed as his daughter; and now he loved her and that was in no way demeaning the love he had had for Siobhan.

He would prove to Marcy, when this was all over, how much she meant to him. He felt a holiday to somewhere warm was calling, something to prepare them for a British winter that was just around the corner.

Chapter 28

BARRY, THERE'S SOMEONE AT the door. Could you get it? I'm not dressed yet," Lisa called out. Barry turned off his electric razor. He looked at his watch. They would have to get a move on if they wanted to catch the first showing at the cinema, and he hurried to answer the doorbell.

"Mr Bartholomew Devlin?" asked the police constable standing on his door step.

"Yes, that's correct, what's the problem?" Barry asked.

"Can we come inside for a few words, please, sir?" asked the policeman, motioning to his colleague standing a few paces behind him.

Barry noticed a female driver in the police car parked on the road as he ushered the two officers into the house. They were quickly joined by Lisa.

"Is there some problem, officers?" she asked as she followed them into the lounge.

"Just confirming if you are the son of Hugh Devlin?" the officer asked.

"Yes, I am. Has anything happened my da? He hasn't been in the best of health lately," replied Barry.

Lisa, sensing the worst, came beside him and took his hand, as the officer explained they had found a body, believed to be that of Hugh, along with another, and that they would need formal identification from Barry or another close relative.

Barry felt his legs go weak and Lisa guided him into a chair. This surely wasn't happening. His mind was working overtime. What did they mean, 'found a body' along with another one?

The officer explained that it seemed to be a killing and a suicide, but nothing had been confirmed yet. Barry and Lisa shook their heads in disbelief.

"Who was the other person?" asked Lisa, and on being informed she screamed, "I told you Barry, there was something creepy about that Liam one, I just knew he was trouble. Oh sweet Mary, mother of Jesus, that bastard has killed Hughie."

On being told it looked as though it might have been Hugh who killed Liam before turning the gun on himself she just looked at them in disbelief. "Bridie, has she been informed?" she sobbed. "That poor woman has just given birth a few weeks ago and has four wee wains to look after. She has been a saint staying with him all these years and putting up with him, but she doesn't deserve this coming to her door step."

"There are officers with her now and they will help her with the children when she goes for the formal identification."

"So what now?" asked Barry "Do I need to go to the station? The morgue? Or what?

"Perhaps you could first come with us to your father's house, just in case there has been anything left there to explain what has happened."

The second office stepped forward, "Lisa, would you like to drive your husband instead of him coming in the car with us. I know how nosy neighbours can be."

"Ack, Jackie, sorry - I didn't recognise you standing there," exclaimed Lisa. "What an introduction to my home and husband." She turned to Barry who had his head in his hands. "This is one of my colleagues from the Musgrave Street station, love."

"Yes," replied Barry. "That's a good idea. If you don't mind, I think a cup of strong tea is called for before we go anywhere. Would you two like one?"

The two officers declined and arranged to meet up at Hughie's house in the next hour. After they'd gone, Lisa put her arms around Barry and cuddled him as a mother would comfort a child. "I'm so sorry, darling, what a terrible shock for you. Come into the kitchen and we'll have a wee cuppa before going to your da's."

She helped him to his feet and led him to the kitchen. She could feel the grief wracking his body. Barry had been so close to his dad in the last few years, making up for all the times he hadn't been in his life when he was growing up.

She vowed to light a candle and ask for strength to help her man through the torment that lay ahead.

Barry was still in a daze when they went inside his father's house.

He could still feel his presence; smell his aroma, as though he had just slipped out for a few minutes. How cruel life could be, he thought, one minute, everything in the garden is rosy and the next the wind taken completely out of your sails.

The first thing he noticed was the envelope on the mantle shelf addressed to himself.

"Is it okay if I open this?" he asked the police officers who had come into the house with them.

"Yes, but we may have to take it away when you have read it, as it could be classed as evidence."

He sat down and Lisa balanced on the arm of his chair and together they read the carefully written note.

"Cancer?" they both questioned simultaneously, shocked looks on their faces.

"He never said he had cancer," mumbled Barry, trying to come to terms with the note's revelation, before reading more.

In the note, Hughie also explained why he was going to 'finish off' Liam. Lisa thought this was an odd way of describing killing one of your oldest friends. There had been enough killings in the name of Ireland, enough was enough. Hughie wrote that 'this was the only way to deal with Liam because his brain was so befuddled with the booze he was incapable of listening to reason.' He was, wrote Hughie, doing Liam's family a favour putting him down.

"For fuck's sake," exclaimed Lisa. "Liam's head wasn't the only one befuddled. It's like he's talking about doing away with an unwanted dog!"

Lisa suddenly realised she never really knew Hughie; how different was he from his peace loving, beautiful minded son.

The note finished off by saying there was another in his coat pocket and it was to be given to whoever was investigating crimes of the past, especially 1972 events. It ended by telling Barry what solicitor was dealing with his will.

"What do you make of that?" asked Barry, handing the note over to Lisa.

She shook her head and then gave the note to her police officer friend Jackie.

"He has mentioned there's another letter in his coat pocket. Do you want us to check?" asked Lisa.

"No need for that, Mrs Devlin," replied Jackie's uniformed colleague. "We found a letter at the scene, and we have this," he said, looking at the note in Jackie's hand. "All we need to do now is arrange a suitable time for Mr. Devlin's body to be identified at the City Morgue, Monday morning suit you okay? I know it's a bit of a wait, but being the week-end..."

"What about Bridie?" asked Lisa. "Is she at the station or at home, poor woman? I think we should call with her, Barry, let her know we care about her."

Jackie said he would check what was happening with Liam's wife and went outside to the patrol car to use the radio. On returning he informed them that their friend Bridie had been admitted to hospital after she'd collapsed in shock. He confirmed she had been taken to the Royal Victoria and advised them to telephone the hospital before visiting.

Barry and Lisa returned home in silence, trying to make some sort of sense of it all. They had so many questions buzzing around in their heads, questions that needed answers; and, how were they going to face their friend Bridie, knowing Hughie had murdered her husband? Would she want to continue being their friend? Would she even speak to them again? Was she aware of the circumstances of Liam's death?

So many questions.

They would have to tread very carefully.

Chapter 29

BRIDIE TOSSED AND TURNED IN her hospital bed. This had to be a dream. What on earth was happening to her? She knew she had asked Hughie to sort things out and, God forgive her, it wasn't the first time she had wished Liam out of her life, but to be murdered; she hadn't thought it would go this far.

She had presumed Hughie would put the fear of God into Liam and warn him off harming the girl he was so intent on 'taking out'. She now felt she had his blood on her hands. It was as though she had hired a hit man. *Oh Mary, Jesus and Joseph...I need a priest.*

A nurse came into the side ward where she lay and proceeded to take her temperature, and to check her blood pressure.

"How are you feeling now, Bridie?" she asked.

Why were nurses like bloody dentists, she thought, and asking questions when your mouth was otherwise engaged?

She grunted and nodded her head. What the nurse was to make of that, who knows, but she seemed satisfied and removed the thermometer from Bridie's mouth, then folded up her blood pressure kit and left the room, saying she would be back soon with a cup of tea.

Bridie tried going over in her head what she had said when last talking to Hughie. She was sure she didn't ask for this outcome. She just wanted Liam put in his place, not six foot under. She just wanted a life of peace and quiet to look after her wee family. That was all that mattered to her, her children.

Oh my God, where are my babies now?

She rang the buzzer that had been placed above her bed, but dozed off before a ward orderly arrived in the room.

"Do you need a bed pan, love, or can you walk to the toilet next door? I've got a wee cup of tea for you. Nurse said you could do with one."

She set the cup on the trolley table across the bed and smiled to herself. Bridie was fast asleep; her sedation was working at last. It was the first she had slept since arriving a few hours ago.

The orderly reached up and reset the buzzer and placed it back near to her hand in case she awoke and needed assistance, lifted the cup and left the ward.

"Bridie is fast asleep," she said as she passed the nurses' station. "Let me know if she wakens and needs a cup of tea, no use leaving this one to get cold."

The nurse thanked her and reading through the notes reckoned it was more than a cup of tea this poor women would need when she woke up to reality; how terrible, her husband murdered and left with four young children, the youngest only a week or two old. When she thought back to the height of the 'troubles' cases like this were the norm and some so much worse, but this wasn't expected now, not in times of peace.

The telephone beside her rang. It was Lisa Devlin enquiring about Bridie and wanting to come and visit. The nurse informed Lisa that Bridie was still in a deep sleep, and told her to ring back in the morning.

Thank goodness she has some friends who care about her, the nurse thought, for she is going to need all the help she can get in the days ahead.

The next call she took was from Musgrave Street R.U.C. station. On the line was the woman police constable who had accompanied Bridie into the hospital. She was given the same information as Lisa and later when the night sister arrived to take over she passed on all the details of their 'special' patient and gratefully went home. It had been a very gruelling day.

Scotland

Pauric telephoned Pearl and got through right away, then realised he had dialled her home number and not the station, so it must be important, he thought, for her to leave her private number with Brian.

She briefly filled him in with the details of the day and said a letter had been left for her, as the only serving member still dealing with any unfinished business from the seventies. He listened intently as she described how the two men had been found and he immediately recognised the names as those Pearl had warned him about a few days ago, the two who could possibly be a danger to Beibhinn.

"What a coincidence, Pearl. These two guys are the ones you were talking about. What on earth happened?"

She told him the contents of the letter and how their fears had been realised. Beibhinn had been recognised as possibly being connected to Siobhan and that Mary, too, (or Ruth, as he knew her) had been spotted by one of the victims. It appeared one of the men had decided to make sure the girls would be safe by shooting the other.

"There was so much more in this letter, Pauric, but too much to detail over the phone. When will you be back in the Province? I think you will find this most interesting."

"I could be back on Monday, Pearl, but Tuesday would suit better as Beibhinn is just getting her head around all the facts of her family's past and she needs more time with Brian. Knowing her, she will want to come back with me that is why I say Tuesday. Will that be okay? And, by the way, do you think it will be safe for her to work over there again? She has this idea in her head of finishing her consignment of duties there and reckons that will take about six months."

"Let's talk about that too when we meet. I think things should be okay for her, but we don't want to take any chances. I don't know how things will pan out here when word gets out about Devlin's death, so let's play it by ear and in the meantime stay close by her side. You'll be thinking you're back on active duty again being a body guard," Pearl laughed. "So, I'll see you on Tuesday. Give me a call when you're on your way and I'll clear my diary for that day."

"That must be some letter you have to divulge if it's going to take all day," mumbled Pauric.

"Be prepared for a major shock. There are some revelations that clear up a lot of mysteries from the past, and some that will affect your friends, and on that note I will bid you good evening," said Pearl.

Chapter 30

LISA STRUGGLED TO REMAIN ASLEEP. From somewhere in the distance the ringing of a telephone was pulling her back to reality and in a semi-conscious state she reached out to the phone on her bedside table. "Lisa Devlin," she muttered, only just audibly.

"Listen up, Lisa Devlin. I will only say this once and you better understand, comprendez?"

Lisa was now fully awake.

"What the hell are you playing at Skinny Magee? Why are you trying to conceal your voice? You are not making a very good job of it. Do you realise it's half past two in the morning?" protested Lisa.

"Right, clever clogs, do as I say and listen! Big Hughie is getting a good old Republican funeral with paras marching and a gun salute to send him on his way; it will be from Clonard and on to Milltown Cemetery, savvy?"

"Right, dick head. You listen to me. My father-in-law is having a private funeral at Roselawn Crematorium with no paramilitary trappings whatsoever, savvy? Let me tell you right now, that was his wish and we shall be fulfilling it. He left notes, you know? If I were in your shoes, instead of making threatening phone calls, I would be high tailing it as far away as possible from this Province. He named and shamed himself and all those connected with him over the years, savvy? If you hear a knock on your door, it won't be opportunity it'll be the peelers coming to get you. Now, do *you* comprendez? Skinny… are you there?"

The disengaged tone told her he had gone and she placed the telephone back on the cradle and cuddled down again under the covers.

Barry stirred beside her. "Was that the 'phone I heard, love? Who was it?"

"No one, darling, just a wrong number," she replied, sleepily.

Chapter 31

BRIAN AND BEIBHINN WERE ALONE in the lounge. Pauric had gone to his room to change for dinner. The rest of the friends had decided to give them some much needed time together, and stayed out of their way.

Sarah popped her head round the door, announcing, "Dinner will be ready in an hour. I will make sure you will not be disturbed in that time, help yourselves to a drink." She pointed over to the drinks cabinet.

Brian waited until Sarah had gone and then took a well-worn envelope from his pocket and passed it over to Beibhinn.

"I think you should read this, love. It was the last correspondence I had from your mother, and it will explain that I never deserted her, far from it, I really wanted her in my life."

"You mean you have kept this letter all of these years?"

asked Beibhinn, taking the fragile piece of paper out of the envelope. Her hands were shaking.

She read it carefully, feeling that she was prying into the secrets of two people very much in love.

"So, you weren't told where exactly she was going and no details of how you could contact her," she stated, looking up from the letter at Brian. "How traumatic this must have been for you both - she, saying goodbye and you, not having the chance to change her mind."

She passed the letter back to Brian. He carefully placed it inside the envelope and then he put it back into his inside jacket pocket.

"That's it in a nutshell, Beibhinn. I never knew of your existence, as my daughter, until very recently. If I had I would have left no stone unturned until I found you both, but that is all water under the bridge and none of us can change the past, only make sure that the future will be good to us both. It won't be easy for either of us, but I feel we will get there in the end. I don't want to lose you out of my life now that I have found you, so let's start building bridges. What say you?"

"Of course, Brian. Sorry but I would find it hard to call you Dad just yet. You are still my friend Brian, step-father to my ex-boyfriend, and speaking of him, won't he be surprised when he hears about all of this!"

"Is there no chance you two will get back together? You seemed a perfect match."

"Not in the foreseeable future. In fact, unless he has a brain transplant I would say it is very doubtful. His perception of married life is the complete opposite of mine."

"Well, they do say opposites attract, Beibhinn, so never say never. I can see me walking you down the aisle yet."

She playfully aimed a cushion at his head, saying, "Perhaps in years to come, with a different groom. At the moment, I want to live a little and travel and, dare I burst your bubble, and say it? Return to Tasmania at the end of my travels."

"Not for a while yet please, Beibhinn. I want us to bond as father and daughter. Now, can this 'learner' father have a hug, please?"

They left for the dining room with arms around each other as Dub came down the stairs, smiling to himself and thinking, *At least things are moving in the right direction.*

As they waited for dinner to be served Brian related his conversation with Pearl McAlister to Pauric and Beibhinn; Marcy joined them.

"Brian, do you want to go with Pauric and Beibhinn on Tuesday? It's been quite a while since you've been across the Irish Sea and it will give you more time to bond with your daughter." At that she gave Beibhinn a hug. "Looks like I'm your step-mum now instead of mother-in-law."

"What about you, darling? I hate to leave you here, having deserted you most of last week," said Brian.

"I have still some paper work to be finalised re the selling of the businesses, I's to dot and T's to cross, too boring for you, my love," replied Marcy. "I will be heading back down to Leeds in the morning, so go on. You know you want to!"

"You will be very welcome to join us," said Pauric, then turning to Beibhinn. "I'm assuming you will be coming too, Miss Beibhinn?"

"Of course, uncle Dub There's no show without Punch. Well dare you leave me out of anything in future!" She pretended to be cross, then started laughing. "I reiterate the welcome, Brian; please say you will come, my treat for lunch on Tuesday. I will introduce you to my favourite eating place, the Bodega, and you must invite Mary along too, uncle Dub."

This comment reminded Pauric that he had yet to telephone Ruth. She must have heard about the shootings by now or maybe not. The news mightn't have yet reached the Press.

Dinner passed over well with all the tensions of the night before truly stored away, Sarah looked around all her family and friends and marvelled that if she hadn't gone on secondment to Northern Ireland all those years ago, what an empty table there would be here now.

It would have been quite possible that she would be sitting alone, a wrinkled old spinster contemplating what might have been, or again, maybe just her and Angus with no Caitlin. She shivered at the thought.

"You cold, hen?" asked Angus, ever watchful and caring for his darling wife.

"No, pet, just someone walking over my grave," she laughed and the others laughed with her.

"Well, let's hope that will not be for many a day, then," her husband said, smiling at her.

Sunday was spent walking by the loch and then having lunch in the village inn. Afterwards, Marcy set off, inviting them all to Leeds as soon as the loose ends had been tied up from this quest.

"Beibhinn's quest," mused Pauric. "That's the main reason we are all together, and I hope a successful quest, Beibhinn?"

"More than I ever imagined, uncle Dub, and I have a feeling it is not over yet. There are still some loose ends, as Marcy calls them, to be sorted."

She raised her glass to her family and friends, yes, she now had a bone fide family and for that she was very grateful.

When they all returned to Glenside, Pauric telephoned Ruth to bring her up to speed on what had happened. He loved the sound of her voice. It was music to his ears after so many years without her. She had heard a news report of the shootings and knew who the victims were, not from the media, but from one of the guys she and Beibhinn had recruited. He had become a very important part of their team.

His father was one of the victims and a friend of his father's the other, but Ruth couldn't remember either of them from her days at Queen's. Apparently, she had been told, they were former paramilitaries and possibly old friends of her late brother.

Ruth agreed to meet for lunch on Tuesday and was looking forward to seeing him again. Feelings that had not surfaced for years were stirring and she was both excited and wary. She did not want to go through the hurt again, the hurt she had suffered on letting this wonderful man leave her life all those years ago. Then again she was not going to deny herself the pleasure of being in his company - that was surely what memories were made of!

Love was what made the world go around, or so all the wordsmiths informed anyone willing to listen, and at this moment in time her world was spinning.

She listened enthralled by his wonderful dulcet tones as he related what had gone on and then spoke of how he was looking forward to meeting her again. She wanted to pull him through the telephone wire and kiss all those words from his velvet lips. She really was getting too involved too quickly. She had to listen to her inner voice of reason.

Never mind my inner voice, she thought, *life is too short and I need this man.*

Reluctantly, they ended their conversation on a promise they would be together very soon. They had 25 years of lost time to make up!

They both fell asleep that night with massive grins on their faces, hoping to dream of each other and the pleasure of the reunion awaiting them.

What would Beibhinn think of him if he spirited her friend back to Tasmania with him? Would she be willing to accompany him this time? His mind was so full of questions, but one thing was for sure, he was not going to let this woman slip out of his life again. Come hell or high water she was going to be his.

Ruth realised he was her destiny, one she had waited for all her life, and slept the sleep of the innocents, not stirring till brought back to life by the intrusion of her alarm clock.

Chapter 32

PAURIC SAT ACROSS THE DESK from Detective Inspector Pearl McAlister, his mouth agape in wonder. "So, you mean to tell me these two stiffs are the same two we discussed last week? Have you any details on why this occurred, and why now?"

"Everything is starting to fall into place, Pauric, but until I get reports back from ballistics it's not an open and shut case. There are quite a few loose ends dangling in the air, but we're working on it and should have some interesting answers very soon."

Pauric stared over at her, waiting for her to continue, but nothing was forthcoming.

"Is that it, then?" he asked. "I thought by our telephone conversation you had a lot more to tell me?"

"I thought by the time you got here I would have had the

ballistics report, but it's taking a little longer than was assumed; it's the history of the weapon that interests me and when I have it confirmed to me, what I suspect from the letter left for me by Hughie Devlin, you will be the first to know. Now, if you don't mind, I will have to get on with other business. We are short a clerical assistant in the office today, who by coincidence is Hugh Devlin's daughter-in-law!"

"Are you happy with that situation? A paramilitary man's daughter-in-law working for the R.U.C.?" he spluttered. "My God, what is the world coming to? Next you'll be telling me some of them will be running for Prime Minister and sitting in Stormont." He laughed at the thought of this.

"Well may you laugh, Pauric. Stranger things have happened in the world, and as for your question about Lisa, she has passed all security checks and a better worker would be hard to find; things are changing here daily, so nothing surprises me anymore."

Pauric left the building and looking up at the Albert Clock decided he would make his way around to the Bodega and join Beibhinn and Brian for a late lunch.

He was feeling a bit peckish with nothing to eat since early breakfast at Glenside before catching the first crossing from Stranraer.

Brian could see so many changes in the city since last being here in the seventies; Beibhinn had parked her car at her apartment and they had walked through the maze of streets to the restaurant. It was one eating establishment he did not remember from his time here, but then he had never socialised much in the city centre.

On the few times they weren't working but having some quality time together, he and Siobhan would have headed into the countryside to a quiet hotel or eating house. He smiled at the thought of the many happy times they had shared together and the very few weekends they tried to be a normal couple just having a break.

It must have been on one of the breaks that Siobhan had conceived, he thought, and remembered all the plans they had made for their future.

"Penny for them," smiled Beibhinn

"Oh my dear all the money in the world could not buy my thoughts today; this is like memory lane for me".

"Did you and Mum come here?" she asked, getting excited at the thought of hearing about Siobhan's early life here in Northern Ireland.

"No, not here in this establishment, but we had a lot of quality time getting to know one another, some of the happiest days of my life." He felt a lump in his throat remembering those past times.

They had just been seated when Pauric joined them.

"My meeting was shorter than I expected, so I thought I would join you both here. Have you ordered yet?"

"Not yet, uncle Dub, we are just about to," replied Beibhinn, smiling at the waitress coming over to their table. "Has Bridie not returned to work yet?" she asked the girl.

The waitress looked around furtively and then sat down with them at the table.

"I'm not one to gossip, Miss," she said to Beibhinn, "but being so good to Bridie in the past you deserve to know; her husband was murdered over the weekend." She was whispering now, looking around and making sure no one else could hear. "His name hasn't been given out yet on the news but it will be probably soon. It will all come out in the wash!"

"Oh my God, I'm so sorry, how is the poor girl coping? What about her children?"

The waitress rose from the seat and made it look as though she had been retrieving something from the floor, and pulling her pen from behind her ear, she said, "Would you like to hear today's specials?" She smiled, and then whispered again, "They are all in foster care, Miss, the poor wee wains, and Bridie is in the Royal Hospital, but I think she is being discharged today, and do you know something else, Miss?" Again she looked around before continuing, "Someone somewhere has done her a big favour, that poor girl deserves some peace in her life." With that she took their orders and walked towards the kitchen.

"Well, is that a coincidence or what?" asked Beibhinn, looking at her two companions. "Could that possibly be connected to that shooting on Saturday you were told about, uncle Dub?"

"It seems very likely, pet. I suppose during the troubles instances like this happened on a daily basis but now are few and far between, so it is very likely there is a connection."

Brian had been listening and wondering how there could be a connection between the husband of a waitress Beibhinn just happened to be acquainted with and a known terrorist who would have known her mother.

There had to be a link somewhere, he thought. Time would tell. Perhaps when Pauric next met with Pearl McAlister things would become a lot clearer.

"Have you been in touch with Ruth, uncle Dub?" asked Beibhinn as she tried to manoeuvre her mouth around the B.L.T. she had ordered. *I swear we are getting very large portions*, she thought. *Perhaps being 'in the know' wasn't such a bad thing.*

"I gave her a call before meeting up here," replied Pauric, blushing. "Hope you don't mind, but I have arranged to take her for dinner this evening and have a long overdue catch up."

"I do believe you are blushing, uncle Dub, don't you agree Brian?" They all laughed as she continued, "It will also give Brian and me a chance to get to know each other better. Would you like to borrow my car?"

"No, pet, you forget I still have the hire car and haven't really got much use out of it what with our trip to Scotland in yours and using 'shank's mare' around the city."

Beibhinn pulled the waitress who had served them to one side as she was leaving the establishment and slipped two twenty pound notes into her hand.

"Please give this to Bridie, and tell her she will be in my prayers. I'm sorry it's not more, but hope it will be of some help to her."

"Ah God bless you, Miss. I will do that, surely I will."

"Are you being a Good Samaritan again, Beibhinn?" asked Dub. "This is Belfast's answer to Mother Theresa," he said to Brian, giving her a hug.

"Have you ever heard the saying, 'What goes around comes around', uncle Dub? Well, that's my philosophy on life and it works for me," she explained with a smile.

How right she was.

Chapter 33

PAURIC LEANED OVER AND MOVED a lock of hair from Ruth's forehead, as she cuddled into his chest. "This is so good," she whispered. "I never thought when leaving Tasmania to come back to Ireland that I would ever see you again, never mind being here with you like this."

He kissed her lips so tenderly as though he was soothing her and letting her know he would protect her through thick and thin. She looked up at him and wanted to pinch herself to make sure this wasn't a dream.

"Are you really here with me, Pauric? Tell me I'm not dreaming." She clung on to him so tightly he could feel his passion rise again.

"Not only am I here, my love, but I swear to you I will never leave you again. I want to take you home with me, far away from all the bad memories you must have here. I never ever want us to be apart. Now that I've found you I will never let you go, so don't even think of disagreeing with me."

She laughed softly and reached up for his lips. She remembered their touch so well when going through the dark periods of her life and it was the memories that had sustained her.

But this, now, wasn't a memory; this was real, and every inch of her body was tingling beside him. He gathered her so close they were as one, the longing in them both needing to be sated.

She kissed his neck and tasted the saltiness. The manly aroma lifted her to heights she had almost forgotten; he was a tender lover, remembering her body so well and knowing exactly how to please her.

There was no rush, they had all the time in the world to please each other and they did, resting now and again only to return to their passion.

Relaxed again, he lay beside her with her head nestling in his arm, his other arm resting softly across her breasts.

"Why have you never married?" he asked. "You must have had admirers through the years?"

"I could ask the same question of you. As for me, no one could ever have taken your place. I focused on my occupation and life hasn't treated me too badly. I just immersed myself in my work and contented myself with the fact I would never marry."

"We are soul mates, darling. I did exactly the same. You were the only woman for me," he said, pulling her round to face him again, "and you still are. I love you so much, my darling."

He kissed her passionately and again she succumbed to his charms, again they went to heaven together, completely in unison.

Then they both fell into a deep sleep of exhaustion, satisfied and totally spent.

Sunshine peeping through the windows forced Pauric's eyes open. It took him a moment or two to focus and recognise his surroundings. The pillow beside him was empty but the space was still warm. He stretched and smiled as Ruth entered the room with two cups on a tray.

"See, I remembered you like coffee with two sugars first thing in the morning," she said as she slipped back into bed beside him, balancing the tray as she did so. He held out his hand to steady the tray as she got comfortable.

He leaned over and kissed her, and said, "Good morning, darling"

They sipped their coffee and she told him she would have to go into the office at some point. With Beibhinn having this week off someone had to cover in case of emergencies. She said she would telephone and let them know she would be late.

"Well, if that is the case," Pauric said, "we better not waste any more time." He took her empty cup, and placed it on the tray before putting it on the floor beside the bed.

She willingly went back into his arms. She felt her pulse rising and passion stirring again. He was also aroused and sensing how much she wanted him, he willingly pleased her, never wanting this feeling to end.

"When will I see you again?" she asked as they dried each other down after their shower.

"How about right now," he playfully teased her as she tried

to get dressed. " I'll stay again tonight, if that's alright by you. We have years to make up for, so how about one more for the road?"

She laughed and gave up all pretence of dressing as he took her there, on top of the towels on her bathroom floor.

"Oh, I love you so much, Pauric, but I will have to go to work. I really will," she said, trying to resist him from pulling her back.

She managed to break free and ran like a two-year-old into the bedroom. He laughingly chased her and they collapsed in a heap on the bed, out of breath and still entwined.

"I think you better phone work and tell them something has come up," she giggled, "and, you won't be able to make it in today."

She pulled him back to where he belonged and whispered, "Yes sir, your wish is my command."

Chapter 34

PAURIC ARRIVED BACK AT BEIBHINN'S apartment and caused some amusement to her and Brian. "Old stop-out!" they chanted in unison.

"Well, I did say we had a lot of catching up to do, and it got to the point it was so late Ruth invited me to stay over," he explained, although the smile on his face said it all.

"This is quite serious then, uncle Dub?" Beibhinn never remembered seeing him this happy; it shone out of him as though the sun had taken residence in his heart.

"I want her to come back with me when I go home, that's how serious it is, darling."

Beibhinn was taken aback. Selfishly she couldn't imagine the office without Ruth and her input was pivotal to the success of the company here in Northern Ireland.

Perhaps she was jumping the gun, perhaps he didn't mean right away.

Brian congratulated Pauric and wished him well with any future plans, and asked when he was going to have the pleasure of meeting this lovely lady who had stolen his friend's heart.

"I'm picking Ruth up from work and we had planned a quiet night in tonight, so how about dinner tomorrow night - all four of us?"

"I feel guilty leaving all the work to Ruth this week of all weeks, perhaps I would be better going back in and letting Ruth have the rest of the week off? What do you think, uncle Dub?"

Pauric explained that until he had the all clear from Pearl about her safety, it would be unwise to go into the office, and how she should take advantage of her time off to spend quality time with Brian. After all, he would be returning to Leeds in a few days' time.

She agreed with him and gave Brian a hug, saying how well their catching up was going and how she loved hearing stories of how her mum and Brian had met, through the community relations team and the fun they had organising events.

Pauric went into the hallway to telephone Pearl. He thought he should have heard from her by now and was impatient to get life back to some sort of normality.

She asked him to come to the station as she didn't want to discuss matters over the phone, so he made his excuses to Beibhinn and Brian and drove the short distance to Musgrave Street.

He made himself comfortable at her desk, feeling like a schoolboy waiting to be reprimanded by the headmaster; it was just the exterior of this building, he thought, that was not very welcoming.

Pearl came into the office carrying two mugs of steaming hot coffee and, using her foot, pushed the door shut.

"Glad you phoned. I have just heard from ballistics and was about to ring you. Glory be - so many questions answered, and you will be delighted with the results too," she revealed, smiling at him.

"Well, missus, don't keep me in suspenders!"

She laughed at his colloquialism.

"The hand gun used to kill Liam and Hughie was the same weapon used on Major Phil all those years ago and on a few others not relevant to this case. It was a sixty-five model Smith and Weston, believed to be one of quite a few caches brought over on the QE2, and before you ask, this happened quite a lot in the seventies. Irish crew smuggled arms on board and at Southampton moved them through to Belfast in small amounts at a time. This was all scuppered by the FBI in the eighties, but who knows how many deaths occurred because of this weak spot in our security."

He shook his head in disbelief, and said, "So, if this was the gun used on Phil, do we know who used it?"

"Oh yes," she replied. "I have a full confession from Hugh Devlin. He was in charge of that little foray, and Liam and Terry Yorke were also on the scene, but were lucky enough to escape our clutches that evening."

"But why the double killing? Did he explain that in his letter?"

"Oh yes, Liam had been at a birthday party for Hugh, in Hugh's son's house and spotted a photograph of Beibhinn and Ruth Yorke, taken alongside Hughie's son. He immediately noticed the likeness to Siobhan and seeing Ruth there, in his fuddled mind, there must have been a connection, so he started making plans. He confided to his wife, more of a boast what he was going to do to both of them, Beibhinn for being related to the traitor Siobhan and Ruth for cutting her brother, his mate Terry, out of her life. Liam's wife Bridie confided in Hugh and the rest is history. He sorted it, and hoping his confession would save his soul, left me a note."

"This Bridie, she wouldn't happen to be a waitress by any chance, would she?"

"That's correct, Pauric Have you been keeping up with your G2 training? What else have you discovered?"

"Beibhinn has been friendly with a waitress in the Bodega. We had lunch there on Tuesday and it was mentioned about her husband being killed, but from what we gathered no tears were being shed - seems like the poor girl didn't have her sorrows to seek. Other than that, I have met up with Ruth again and I want her to remain in my life. This case wrecked our relationship all those years ago, so I am hoping now that it had resurged it will set the relationship with strong cement."

They continued talking and going into details about the outcome, and Pearl was so pleased she could now finalise so many unsolved cases taking up room in the files. She told him how happy she was for him and divulged she had also met up with a friend from the past and he was arriving from England this evening. She was picking him up from the City Airport and if he didn't mind she wanted to go home to change before then.

Pauric suggested they all meeting up for dinner the next evening as more of a celebration and reunion of old friends. She readily agreed and he said he would get Beibhinn to book a table at the Dirty Duck in Holywood.

When he returned to the apartment and began to relate the

conversation with Pearl, Brian's reaction was to phone Marcy and tell her Phil's tormentor and perpetrator was now dead and how he was looking forward to coming home to her.

Beibhinn, on the other hand, was amazed at how small a world they lived in, how all the coincidences had come together. Yes, she thought, truth was stranger than fiction.

She was delighted to be meeting Pearl tomorrow night, and looked forward to hearing how she and Siobhan had travelled to Australia together. She relished hearing anything about her mother's past. so she happily booked a table for six at the Dirty Duck.

Pauric took his leave, saying he was collecting Ruth from the office and heading back to Holywood. They arranged to meet the next evening at seven in the lounge bar of the establishment, leaving Beibhinn to plan a day out together with her dad, taking in the sights and a stroll down some memory lanes.

Chapter 35

THE DRIVE TO HOLYWOOD FROM Belfast along the Sydenham bypass was a trip down memory lane for Brian. Beibhinn had insisted on driving and he was able to take in the scenery at his leisure.

"Not a lot has changed here," he observed, "since the days I travelled out and about from Palace Barracks."

"Are you having some déjà vu moments, Brian?" she asked, smiling at him.

As they parked the car at the Dirty Duck, Pearl and her companion were alighting from a taxi just ahead of them. Brian did a double take. Yes he was expecting Pearl, a figure from his past, but no way was he prepared for the pleasant surprise at recognising her companion. Pearl smiled and held out her hand to Brian who was a few steps ahead of Beibhinn.

"Good to see you again, Brian, and under a lot more pleasant circumstances," he said, taking her hand and pulling her towards him to give her a hug.

"Good to see you too, Pearl, and what a surprise. How are you, Joe? What a dark horse! You keeping Pearl a secret from your old mate?" he asked in jest, shaking hands with his old colleague.

Beibhinn stood looking on in amusement. She thought in his excitement Brian had forgotten she was with him. She stepped towards Pearl and introduced herself. Pearl in turn introduced her to Joe and together they proceeded to the restaurant to meet up with Pauric and Ruth.

The three men had so much catching up to do that the ladies felt quite redundant, but the chat flowed freely and there were no awkward silences.

"How did you and Joe meet up?" enquired Beibhinn.

Pearl explained she had been on a training course in Leeds just over a year ago and literally bumped into Joe while shopping. They hadn't seen each other since the seventies when they had both been involved in the Major's case, and arranged to meet up for dinner that evening, and they had been together ever since.

Joe had been a widower for four years and she a widow for twenty and they enjoyed each other's company, albeit from a distance most of the time. They tried to catch up as often as possible, when their respective jobs allowed.

Pearl and Ruth both agreed how alike Beibhinn was to her mother Siobhan, and soon all six were chatting away, remembering how things were back in 'the old days'. Beibhinn absorbed every bit of information with relish, if only her mum were alive to know how small the world had become.

Pauric announced that Ruth had agreed to come to Tasmania and, seeing the look of shock on Beibhinn's face, explained she would finish her task here first and hope for a transfer to the Hobart office along with Beibhinn.

"I have asked my Ruth, your Mary," he said, smiling at Beibhinn, "to marry me and she has made me the happiest guy in the world by saying yes!"

Beibhinn was delighted. She couldn't have wished for a better person to come into uncle Dubs life. He made Ruth blush when he recalled his first days at HT 1212 and how he had drove the other jocks mad at his continuous playing of Nilsson's 'With or Without You'.

He had them all laughing when he told them how the vinyl record was now smooth; all the grooves had gone.

"Well, I will hunt about in some music shops to find a copy of that song, have it framed and present it to you two as a wedding gift."

Ruth blushed at Beibhinn's remark, but inwardly loved the feeling of being Pauric's wife.

"Well, all's well that ends well," said Brian. "Looks like we have all done well for ourselves, after all those the turbulent years. I think we should have a toast to our futures."

They all clinked glasses. *To the future.*

Beibhinn said it was a shame Sarah, Angus, Caitlin and Steven couldn't be here. Pauric said they would have plenty of time for that when they all got together for his wedding to his darling Ruth.

"Where's it to be then, uncle Dub, and when?" asked Beibhinn.

"Well, I've been telling Ruth – or shall we call her Mary from now on - all about the little village we went to last week, Luss? I was going to 'phone Sarah and see if she could help organise something there for us; the wee church where her aunt and uncle are buried would be the ideal setting and she would know of the best place to hold the reception. What do you think, Beibhinn?"

"I think the first thing she will do, knowing Sarah, is to offer Glenside as the perfect place for your reception. How many guests are you thinking of?"

Ruth interceded, "Just all those present here plus the Scottish people. We want it to be quiet and intimate, so ten plus us makes a perfect dozen."

"Well, good luck uncle Dub with the organising and I know Sarah will be more than willing to help."

Brian stood up, and said, "I think we should toast our absent friends, including my Marcy. I can't wait to see her tomorrow."

"Talking of tomorrow, I have a funeral to attend," said Ruth, and looking at Beibhinn continued, "Barry's father's funeral is tomorrow, so I will be going to represent the firm, not that I relish the idea but needs must. We have to show respect to Barry; he is proving to be a very reliable colleague."

"His wife work's in my office," said Pearl, "but, under the circumstances we have sent a sympathy card. I don't think it would look too good for a serving officer to attend an old rebel's funeral, irrespective of the fact it would be to show support for his daughter-in-law. However, another civilian clerk will be representing the office, Joanne. She actually recommended Lisa for the position when it became vacant and Lisa sailed through the interview and as she had already passed her civil service tests we offered her the job, and she has become a very valuable member of the team."

On that rather sobering thought the friends said they would keep in touch, before going their separate ways.

Dub said he would take Brian to the airport the next morning, as he had to return his hire car before noon, so could kill two birds with one stone. Beibhinn agreed to collect him from the airport and explained that she would bring him back to make those all-important calls to Sarah regarding the wedding.

Oh, there was going to be some exciting times ahead, she thought, relishing the idea of Ruth joining the family and returning home to Tasmania with her and uncle Dub.

Chapter 36

IT WAS A BLEAK AUTUMN morning as Johnny looked out through his bedroom window. It had rained heavily all through the night. Typical Belfast weather, he thought, the type of overcast morning his old mother would have called 'a day for a hanging'. He pulled his funeral suit out from the back of the wardrobe and continued dressing.

He negotiated the stairs and looked at his image in the full length mirror on the way down. Beside the mirror was a brass ornamental plaque with a clothes brush and shoe horn hanging side by side.

He removed the brush and carefully brushed his shoulders and sleeves before replacing it back onto the plaque.

He straightened his black tie and thought, *don't want to be disrespectful to my old mate.*

"Maggie, did you order a taxi for me?" he shouted in the direction of the kitchen.

"No need to shout, yes I did, but here get this into you," she said and passed a steaming cup of tea to him. "This will keep the chill out of you at the cemetery. What a bleak windy place Roselawn will be today, nearly as bad as the graveyard at Carnmoney, although why you choose to go at all is beyond me."

"All graveyards can be bleak in the rain," he replied, "and, you well know Hughie and me have been friends since childhood, so no way would I stay away. I want to pay my respects."

"A man from the Shore Road and an old Provo, friends? Who on earth would believe it? I only hope some of the wee eejits from around here don't get wind of it or God alone knows what we would have to put up with."

"Maggie, you worry over nothing. You're like a dog with a bone. Hughie was an ex Provo, just like me, past our sell-by dates, and unless you open your gob, who will know where I'm off to today?"

No such thing as an ex paramilitary, thought Maggie. Once in, in for life. Surely Johnny knew that.

The only reason his skills, if he ever had any, were no longer used was his age, well past his best, thank the good Lord, although when she thought about it, he had been a wee bit flush over the last few years since the ceasefire.

She knew better than to question Johnny as to where the extra money had come from, and hadn't she enjoyed a wee break to Benidorm with him, maybe on the spoils of 'dirty money'?

Life was so much better between them now. When she thought back to the past and how hard the times were it made her shiver, although she had to laugh at some of his antics when he was younger.

She remembered her mother asking her if she was wise in the head, marrying a man who rode up and down the Shore Road on a horse thinking he was Roy Rogers instead of just plain Johnny Rogers.

No, there was nothing plain about her Johnny. He had been a good husband to her, well, when he wasn't keeping his friends company at Her Majesty's pleasure.

Even during those times, she was well looked after by the 'prisoners wife and children fund'. In fact, a lot better off than when he was at home.

"That's my taxi now, love. I'll be home before six, and then maybe you would like to go up to Glengormley to the cinema? We haven't done that for a while, and I'll bring us two fish suppers home for tea."

The taxi driver was quiet. Johnny didn't relish talking about the reason for his journey to Roselawn and perhaps the cabbie realised that people going to funerals didn't really want to talk about football and other interesting subjects on the half hour journey.

"If you drop me off at the gates on the Ballygowan Road that will do me fine," Johnny said to the driver as they neared their destination. He realised he was a half hour early going by the times in the Belfast Telegraph and Irish News and thought a walk through the cemetery to the crematorium would clear his head.

So many headstones, he though, as he wandered through the walkways. *I guess I have more friends here and in Carnmoney than I have left here on earth.*

One name on a headstone drew his attention on a well-tended grave: *Best... In loving memory of Annie M...beloved wife and mother.*

This was the final resting place of the mother of George Best, the Belfast boy, and best ever Northern Ireland footballer of his generation, loved by Manchester United fans the world over.

Johnny paused at the graveside and then made his way towards the crematorium and on in through the floral tribute hall, where he checked under the name plaque for Hugh Devlin. Sure enough, there was his floral tribute.

He had not put his name. He had told the florist to sign it 'from a childhood friend' and to add the words of an old Belfast adage 'Keep Her Lit'.

On reading it now he wondered if the wording was entirely appropriate. He had meant it in relation to their tobacco runs, but at a crematorium! He suppressed a nervous laugh and knew Hughie would see the funny side.

He went into the main hall and sat in the back row of the pews. The coffin was straight ahead, and as he looked around this small intimate room he noticed there weren't many others attending.

Ahead of him in the front row sat Barry and his wife Lisa along with Hughie's sister Betty and her husband Jim. Behind them were Hughie's niece Monica and her current flame, and beside them was Bridie.

Barry came to her and thanked her for coming and noticed how pale this poor girl looked. She had enough on her plate organising Liam's funeral and here she was, a true friend to him and Lisa.

Ruth sat behind them, beside Joanne, and they said they would catch up after the service.

Less than a dozen people to see him off, thought Johnny, as he tried to look as inconspicuous as possible. After Barry had said a few words, the coffin was lowered out of view, and Johnny took this opportunity to quietly slip out of the door and make his way home.

Barry, meanwhile, invited those present to join him and Lisa for coffee and refreshments in the Reflections coffee shop beside the crematorium.

Ruth and Joanne hadn't seen each other since their time at Queen's University and it was good to catch up. They had been friends then. It was as though the years had just slipped away and they exchanged telephone numbers and vowed to keep in touch.

Bridie pulled Barry to the side and told him she did not hold any grudges over Liam's death. She felt as though she had been released from purgatory and said she always knew Liam would come to a bad end. He thanked her and Lisa joined them, giving Bridie a hug and telling her they would always be there for her.

As they all made their way home, the skies had cleared and a large rainbow formed over the city, as if promising it a peaceful future.

Only time would tell.

About the Author

Shirley Gault was born in Belfast and educated at Carr's Glen Primary school and Belfast Royal Academy.

The mother of two was widowed in 2007 when her husband passed away; he had been suffering from Parkinson's disease and Lewy Body dementia for the last 18 years of his life.

Shirley is no stranger to listeners of local radio in her native Northern Ireland, having a regular and popular poetry reading slot.

She began by writing Valentine's Day rhymes for friends before having her first poetry published. Her style has been described as 'romantic,' and she says that being a 'people person and people watcher' enables her to cover love in all its forms – love of people, love of places and love of life.

The following pages contain some of her poetry from *Reflections & Reflections Two*...

MEMORIES OF 60'S BELFAST

In the swinging 60's Belfast was the place to be,

With clubs galore and even more

So many stars to see.

With Tony Morelli at the Piccadilly line,

At Titos and The Talk of the Town was Candy Devine.

At the Abercorn, the resident crew

Were George Jones and Clubsound with comedy too.

John Cooke was a great compere, as was Roy Walker,

They kept us enthralled with their quirky wit,

John was a smooth talker.

The show bands delighted the dancers

At the Orpheus, Fiesta and Floral Hall,

With the Miami, Cadets and Dickie Rock

The fans really had a ball.

Chicken in a basket was a snack time pleasure

As we watched the stars perform,

Ah memories to treasure,

No one was ever forlorn.

Then the 'Troubles' took over the city,

For thirty years and more,

The music died, oh what a pity,

to see each venue close its door.

Now peace has returned to Belfast,

The dancing has started again.
We all pray this peace will last,
Let the buzz in the city remain.

MY LIFELONG FRIEND

Like a gladiator you took the shield
And fought with all your might,
Invading monsters you battled,
Round one went to you in the fight.

As the months passed by you rested,
Surrounded by family love,
Knowing soon you would be tested,
Gathered strength from up above.

You lived each day to the full,
Inspired all those around,
Your cheerfulness kept hidden, doubts,
You uttered not a sound.

But now the final battle
Has turned into a war,
Invasion from every quarter,
Leaving you worn out and sore.

You fought a good fight,
From beginning to end,

And now God knows best,

My precious friend.

Now you're free from pain,

Rest my little Beauty,

Rest my lifelong friend

Till we meet again.

PERFECT TIMING

When is it time to say good-bye?

When do the eyes cease to cry?

When does a broken heart repair the strain?

When do the skies turn to blue again?

Enough is enough

Cries the aching brain,

It's time to live

For yourself again.

Life goes by

At so fast a pace,

Don't waste anymore time,

Give yourself space.

Though painful now

You must go on,

Say your goodbyes

Greet a fresh new dawn.

In time, the hurt

Will cease to be,

Store all away

In your memory.

When it's safe

To look back and view,

You'll be glad you decided,

To start anew.

CHINK OF HOPE

Your air of bravado

Hiding your shyness

Doesn't fool me;

Your smiling eyes

Betray the sadness of your lips.

Your 'couldn't care less' attitude

Masks a deeply caring nature;

You have been hurt so much in your past

That you have had to build a guard

To prevent being hurt again.

Your true persona is buried deep

Behind a façade, so unlike the real you.

You fear love,

You think it can only bring heartache and pain,

Your self-esteem is so low

You refuse to believe you can be loved,

And revered by anyone, ever again.

The tiny chink in your armour,

Gives me hope,

Please let this grow into a gaping chasm,

One that I can penetrate,

Then perhaps you will be convinced,

You are capable of loving, and being loved,

For the truly beautiful person you are.

BETRAYAL

Friendship is the strongest bond

Between two people,

It has to be earned

It can't be bought.

To betray a friendship

Is a despicable act,

It can cause more pain

Than a knife to the heart.

A true friendship

Is a God given gift,

Cherish it well

Never abuse for personal gain.

Once the chain is broken

A link will be missing,

Repair will be impossible,
It will never be the same.

Be careful with difficult choices,
The outcome could sever
The strongest bond
You will ever know.

Among other books currently available from David J Publishing:

Another Time Another Place
By Shirley Gault

She was visibly shaken. Angus her dearest friend was in love with her! She really did love him too, but not in a romantic way, more as a brother. Oh no, please do not let this be happening, she thought.

'Another Time Another Place' is the first published collection of short stories from the author of the much praised books of poetry, **'Reflections' & 'Reflections Two.'**

The collection includes **'The Warder's Daughter,'** an autobiographical account, dedicated to the memory of her loving parents, Mary and Albert, which focuses on the dilemmas and delights of growing up in Belfast in the 1960s.

"My inspiration can come from a single word or a beautiful sunset; nature's inspiration is endless," says Shirley, who was born in Belfast and educated at Carr's Glen Primary and Belfast Royal Academy.

Santa Fe Sisters
by Colin McAlpin

It is the late 1880s. Sisters Georgina and Violet Sophia Devonshire live in the village of Glenscullion in the beautiful Glens of Antrim in Northern Ireland enjoying a life of good fortune, until misfortune befalls them and they are forced to leave for a new, yet uncertain, life in America.

On the voyage from Londonderry to Baltimore they befriend an elderly gentleman who unfortunately dies during the journey. It is an encounter that changes their lives forever. Along the way, the sisters meet a collection of weird and wonderful characters, including a deadly business rival, a colourful vaudeville singer and an enigmatic preacher man. And romance may be on the cards too. But will their dreams turn to reality in the face of opposition, danger and betrayal?

SANTA FE SISTERS is a carefully researched story featuring strong female characters who will keep you enthralled until the very last page; it's a tale that will linger long in the memory and leave you wanting more.

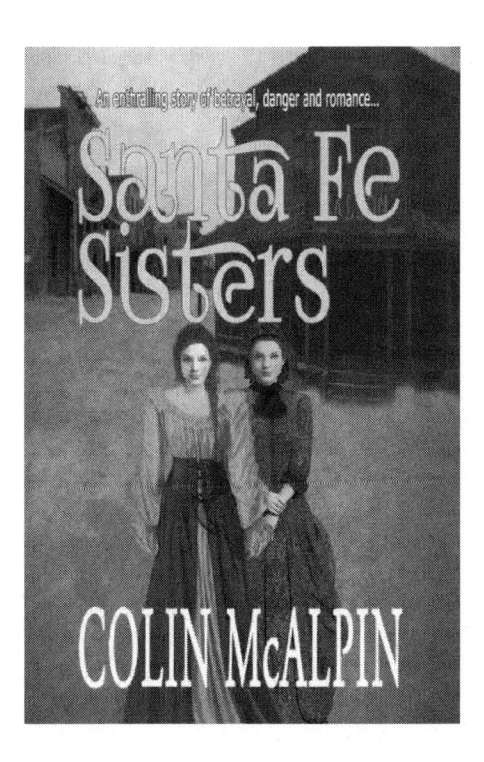

Trying Times
By Janice Donnelly

This is an enlightening and touching story of how you can still come out smiling despite all the trials and tribulations of life.

Take Cassie; she is holding down three jobs to make ends meet. Then there is Jo; she is struggling with university and part time work, while friend, Gail, faces up to the prospects of redundancy.

Meanwhile, young and beautiful Orla appears to have it all, but appearances are deceptive. And with his sixtieth birthday looming, Benny and his wife Deirdre are looking forward to a new found freedom, until a phone call changes all that.

This is a multi-layered contemporary tale that will sometimes bring a smile to your face and other times a tear to your eye. Set in a Northern Ireland that is finally at peace – well, almost – *Trying Times* focuses on the strength and importance of relationships in difficult circumstances, taking up where the author's well received debut novel *Buying Time* left off…

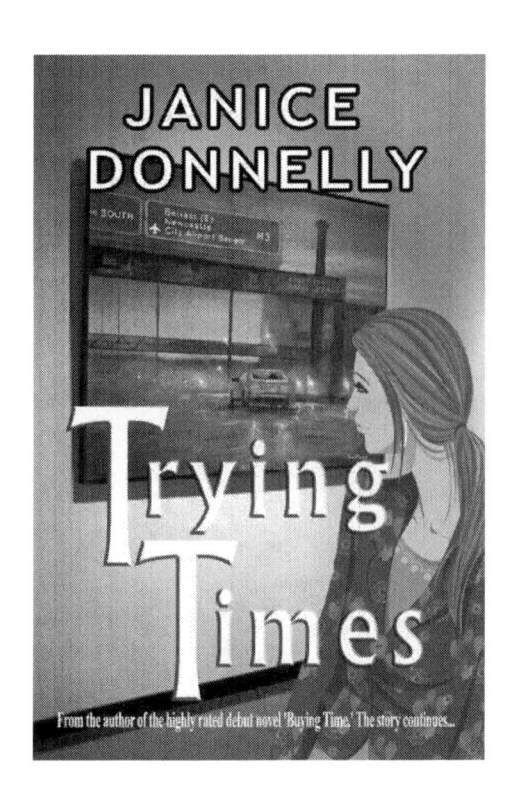